"Keep talking," Nick insisted, going closer. "First, put that gun away."

She looked down at the Glock, and as Nick had done earlier, she seemed to have a debate about whether or not she should do that. A quick debate. Because only seconds later, Hallie tucked the gun into the back waistband of her jeans. Into a slide holster, no doubt. When she'd been on the job, that'd been where she'd kept her backup weapon, with her primary in a shoulder holster similar to his.

With the threat of the Glock gone, Nick relaxed just a little.

However, he made sure he kept his eyes pinned to her.

Which was something that often happened whenever he'd been around Hallie.

Of course, those other times weren't because she'd pulled a gun on him, but rather because of the tug of attraction that had always been there between them.

And always forbidden.

LAWMAN TO THE CORE

USA TODAY Bestselling Author

DELORES FOSSEN

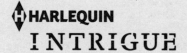

HARLEQUIN®
INTRIGUE™

ISBN-13: 978-1-335-58234-8

Lawman to the Core

Copyright © 2022 by Delores Fossen

Recycling programs for this product may not exist in your area.

For questions and comments about the quality of this book, please contact us at CustomerService@Harlequin.com.

Harlequin Enterprises ULC
22 Adelaide St. West, 41st Floor
Toronto, Ontario M5H 4E3, Canada
www.Harlequin.com

Printed in U.S.A.

Delores Fossen, a *USA TODAY* bestselling author, has written over one hundred novels, with millions of copies of her books in print worldwide. She's received a Booksellers' Best Award and an RT Reviewers' Choice Best Book Award. She was also a finalist for a prestigious RITA® Award. You can contact the author through her website at www.deloresfossen.com.

Books by Delores Fossen

Harlequin Intrigue

The Law in Lubbock County

Sheriff in the Saddle
Maverick Justice
Lawman to the Core

Mercy Ridge Lawmen

Her Child to Protect
Safeguarding the Surrogate
Targeting the Deputy
Pursued by the Sheriff

Visit the Author Profile page at Harlequin.com.

CAST OF CHARACTERS

ATF agent Nick Brodie—He's faced danger before, but the stakes are sky-high when he protects a former agent and the baby she's adopting.

Hallie Stanton—After nearly being killed in the line of duty, she has started a new life, but that's threatened when someone goes after her child.

David—Rescued from a militia's black market baby ring, he's too young to know the danger around him.

Ty Levine—A handyman who was once involved with David's biological mother. He could know more than he's saying about who's after the baby.

Lamar Travers—A member of the militia who's missing, but he could be working behind the scenes to kidnap David and eliminate anyone trying to protect him.

Darius Lawler—A criminal informant with ties to the militia. He claims his life is in danger, but it could be a ruse to draw out Nick and Hallie.

Steve Fain—A former ATF agent who was in on the raid of the militia the night David was rescued, but was he actually running the black market baby ring?

Chapter One

Special Agent Nick Brodie heard the sound that he didn't want to hear when he went inside his house. As usual, he'd come in through the garage entrance, past the mud room and then into the kitchen. Also as usual, he'd stopped for a heartbeat.

And just listened.

It was something Nick had made a habit of doing after a decade of being in law enforcement. It was the first time though in the decade that the stopping and listening had allowed him to hear someone moving around. Someone who definitely shouldn't be here since he lived alone, and he was the only one with a key to the place.

Everything inside him went on alert, and he reached for the gun in his shoulder holster, the metal whispering against the leather as he drew it. But it was already too late.

"Don't," the *someone* warned him in a hoarse whisper. It was a woman. "Keep your hands where I can see them. I've got a Glock aimed at you."

Because Nick didn't know if that was an actual threat

or a bluff, he did as she'd said. He didn't especially want to get gunned down tonight in his own home. However, he also didn't plan to have a weapon trained on him for long. Somehow, he'd put a stop to this.

Whatever *this* was.

Nick lifted his hands in the air. Just a little, and he kept his hand at the right angle that he'd need if he had to dive to the side and fire his own Glock. He turned, picking through the nearly dark living and kitchen area so he could try to spot his visitor.

The only illumination came from the clock on the microwave and the watery moonlight slanting in through the bay window over the sink. The intruder was on the side of his fridge, her face concealed in the shadows. He couldn't see her features, but he could estimate that she was about five-six. No need for him to guess or estimate whether or not she was truly armed because the moonlight glinted off the barrel of her gun.

Nick considered ID'ing himself, letting her know that he was a special agent with the Bureau of Alcohol, Tobacco, Firearms and Explosives, but he doubted that would be news to her. After all, she had come here to his house in Lubbock, had broken in and then had lain in wait for him. A burglar would have just robbed the place and left. It was his guess that she knew exactly who and what he was.

And that meant whatever this was had to be related to the badge.

Maybe this woman had some kind of score to settle

with him over an investigation? Or she could be evading arrest with the hopes of using him in some way to do that. Hell, maybe she just hated lawmen and had thought this was the best way to take one out.

"What do you want?" he demanded, making sure there was plenty of that lawman's tone in his question.

"I want you to holster your gun. Then, you can tell me if you're responsible for what happened today," she answered. No hesitation, either, and this time, she didn't whisper so Nick had no trouble recognizing her voice.

Hallie Stanton.

Hell's bells. What the devil was she doing here?

Nick had thought knowing the name of the intruder would tell him why she was holding him at gunpoint. But it didn't. It'd been a while since he'd seen or heard from this former ATF agent who had once worked for him. Six months and eight days to be exact. Hard not to remember because that's when both of them had come damn close to dying.

"Put your gun away," Hallie ordered, sounding very much like the agent she'd once been.

He debated it. And decided to do as she'd demanded. However, Nick kept his hand over his Glock once it was back in the shoulder holster.

"Are you responsible for what happened today?" she snapped.

Nick huffed, shook his head. "You're going to need to give me a little more than that, Hallie. Because I don't have a clue what you're talking about."

She echoed the sound and adjusted her aim. Away from his heart. And toward his head. Apparently, she hadn't cared much for his response. *Welcome to the club.* There was plenty about this situation—including her own lack of answers—that riled Nick to the core.

"Lower your gun, and we'll talk." Nick kept his gaze pinned to hers. What he could see of her anyway. And he took a step closer. Just as something else occurred to him. Something bad. "What happened to you today? Does it have anything to do with the last case we worked together?" A black market baby ring they'd busted.

"Bingo." There was plenty of sarcasm, as if she believed he knew that was exactly what this was about.

Nick didn't especially want to go through the events of that particular bust. Definitely not his finest hour. Partly because he hadn't known there was an illegal baby operation until after Hallie, he and the rest of their team had gained entry into a militia compound where there'd been reports of stockpiled weapons. There'd been weapons all right. Plenty of them. But there'd also been seventeen babies, ranging in age from a newborn to just under a year.

The images of those tiny babies were etched in his mind. So were the details that had emerged. Because all seventeen babies had been kidnapped, bought or birthed with surrogates for hire, and all had been in the process of being sold. Maybe to people desperately wanting a shortcut to parenthood. Maybe not. Nick doubted the militia leader would have been too picky when it came to whoever was paying up to fifty grand to get a healthy child.

The ATF team had stopped the black market operation and had even managed to reunite all but one of the babies with their parents or relatives. But it hadn't been an easy victory.

And both Hallie and he had the scars from the bullet wounds to prove it.

They'd survived what had turned out to essentially be an ambush. *Barely* survived. And afterward, after the doctors had fixed what they could, Nick had returned to duty. Not Hallie though. She'd turned in her badge and left the ATF to start her own private investigator business in the nearby small town of Dark River. Nick knew that because his brother lived there.

"I'm sorry you got shot that night," he said. "I was the team leader so I take full responsibility." But Nick didn't think she'd come here for an apology. No. Something else was going on. If she'd wanted revenge for the shooting, she would have come after him sooner than this. "I didn't stay in touch with you, but I'm guessing you're still dealing with the aftermath of the injury."

It wasn't a question. Of course, she was dealing with it and the PTSD. Being shot in the line of duty came with a boatload of aftermath. That's why he was surprised when Hallie shook her head.

"This isn't about me getting shot," she snarled. "It's about the break-in at my house. It's about me being stalked. *Hunted.* It's about the whereabouts of an innocent woman," she added, her voice hitching. "I want to know why and what part you played in all of that."

Nick was reasonably sure if she'd given him a multiple choice about why she was there, he wouldn't have guessed anything she'd just said.

"Stalked? Hunted?" he repeated, and he immediately thought to call the sheriff of Dark River, Leigh Mercer. It was late, already past nine, but since Leigh was engaged to his brother, Nick figured she wouldn't mind a business call during nonbusiness hours. First though, he wanted a few more facts from Hallie.

"How are you being stalked and hunted?" he pressed.

"Someone wants me dead," Hallie insisted. "And I want you to tell me what you know about that."

Nick sighed and tried to rein in his impatience. Hard to do though when this wasn't making sense. "Why don't you start from the beginning?" he suggested. But it was more than a mere suggestion. It was a necessity. "Because I don't have a clue what you're talking about."

The breath she dragged in was long, weary and doused in raw nerves. Strange, since he'd always thought of Hallie as having nerves of steel. She certainly had nothing but steel during the five years they'd worked together.

Hallie stepped out from the fridge a little, glancing first down at the floor to her right. Just a glance. Before her gaze whipped back to his.

She was wearing jeans and a blue top and had her dark brown hair pulled back. Nick could see her eyes now. Hard and focused. But there was something else stirring in all those shades of green. Fear.

Not good.

Because scared, desperate people didn't often make wise choices. It wasn't wise for her to keep pointing that gun at him. Even if she didn't have actual plans to kill him, she could end up accidentally pulling the trigger.

"Tell me what's wrong," Nick said. He didn't move closer and kept his voice as calm and level as he could manage.

"What's wrong," she spat out, "is that Veronica Richards is missing." A hoarse sob tore from her throat. "Missing and maybe dead."

The name meant nothing to Nick, but apparently it meant plenty to Hallie. "She was a friend? If so, I can help you find her—"

"Not a friend," Hallie said, cutting him off. "She's David's foster mother." Again, she studied his expression. Then, she frowned. "You really don't know?" She sounded as surprised, and puzzled, as he was.

"I really don't know," Nick assured her, hoping that this time she'd actually believe him. "Who's Veronica Richards and David?"

The question had no sooner left his mouth though when he recalled reading a report. One that'd been finalized a couple of weeks after the bust of the black market baby ring. DNA testing had made it possible to ID all but one of the babies.

A boy that social services had named David.

There'd been no DNA match so they couldn't ID his parents, or any kin for that matter, and no one had reported a missing infant matching his description.

"David went into foster care," Nick said, filling in the blanks. "I'm guessing foster care with this woman, Veronica Richards? What happened to them?" Before she could answer though, Nick amended that. "What happened to you to make you come here tonight?"

Hallie continued to stare at him, and then she muttered something that he didn't catch. "Veronica thought you might be part of this. Part of the illegal baby operation," she added.

Now, it was Nick's turn to mutter, but his was profanity, and he darn sure didn't keep it under his breath. He cursed plenty loud enough for Hallie to hear. "I don't even know Veronica." But that would soon change. First chance he got, he'd run a full background check on the woman. "Why would she think I had anything to do with the baby ring?"

Hallie opened her mouth. Quickly closed it. And she sighed. She also lowered her gun. "An anonymous tip."

Nick didn't appreciate his name being bandied about by some idiot trying to smear his reputation and his badge. Especially someone hiding behind anonymity. But why would this person have made the accusation about him in the first place? Better yet, why would Veronica and Hallie have believed it? There was nothing in his record or background to make anyone think he was dirty. Because he wasn't. Never had been, never would be.

"Keep talking," Nick insisted, going closer. "First though, put that gun away."

She looked down at the Glock, and as Nick had done earlier, she seemed to have a debate about whether or not she should do that. A quick debate. Because only seconds later, Hallie tucked the gun into the back waistband of her jeans. Into a slide holster, no doubt. When she'd been on the job, that'd been where she'd kept her backup weapon with her primary in a shoulder holster similar to his.

With the threat of the Glock gone, Nick relaxed just a little. However, he made sure to keep his eyes pinned to her. Which was something that often happened whenever he'd been around Hallie. Of course, those other times wasn't because she'd pulled a gun on him but rather because of the tug of attraction that had always been there between them.

And always forbidden.

Because she'd worked for him, Hallie had been hands-off. And despite the mutual heat, Nick hadn't broken the rules, but that hands-off would have ended when she'd quit the bureau if she hadn't left Lubbock.

"Have you heard from Steve Fain recently?" she asked.

Again, she'd surprised him. Steve had also once worked for Nick, but Steve, too, had quit the ATF shortly after Hallie. "No. Why?"

"Because he's the one who first came to me and told me there was a problem, that he thought there'd been a cover-up with the black market baby ring investigation."

This was the first Nick was hearing about a cover-up, but there had been questions as to why the intel the ATF had been gathering inside the militia hadn't given them a heads-up about the babies being kept there.

"Why does Steve think there was a cover-up?" Nick demanded. "And what does that have to do with you being here?"

She dragged in another long breath, and this one was heavy with frustration. "I think it has everything to do with my situation. For days now, I believe someone's been following me, and I found an eavesdropping device in my car."

Okay, so Hallie had been right about the stalking. "You're a PI," he said. "Maybe it's connected to one of your cases?"

"I don't have any active cases. I do research and background checks for some larger PI agencies." She paused a heartbeat. "A couple of hours ago, someone broke into my home. The person who did that jammed my security system. *A top-notch security system*," she said with emphasis.

Nick figured he knew where this was going. "And you thought I'd done that because I know how to jam alarms?"

"I thought a cop or someone in law enforcement could have done it," Hallie corrected him. "I was in my bedroom when I saw a guy in a ski mask step into the doorway. He was armed and was carrying duct tape and rope, so I don't think he had friendly intentions."

Nick wanted to curse again. Even for a former agent, having someone break in like that had to be a nightmare.

"Since I was spooked about being followed and finding the bug in my car," she continued, "I'd put my gun on the nightstand. I grabbed it, and the guy ran. He left behind a baby blanket and a pacifier in the living room. Things that I'm sure he planned on using to take David." She paused again. "I had David with me at my house."

Nick had been following the explanation just fine until she said that. "You had the baby with you?" he asked, more than a little surprised. "Why?"

"Veronica gave me permission to take him for the night since I'm having David's custody transferred to me. I'm in the process of adopting him."

Nick had definitely missed out on any talk about that. He'd never heard Hallie say anything about wanting to be a parent, but it was possible that she'd gotten close to the child because of the ordeal they'd both been through.

"Where's David now?" Nick asked.

She motioned to the floor by the fridge where he'd seen her glance a couple of times. Nick went closer, peering over the waist-high partial wall that divided the kitchen from the living area.

And there was the baby, sleeping in an infant seat.

Hell. David had been here the whole time that Hallie

had been aiming a gun at him. That told Nick just how desperate and frightened she was.

Nick stared down at the baby. He'd certainly grown in these six months, but he still had the thick black hair that Nick remembered.

A dozen things went through Nick's head. Not good things, either. David had been with Hallie when that masked intruder had bypassed her security system and broken in. Having the baby with her would have added several extra layers of terror to an already terrifying situation.

"You've reported this to Sheriff Leigh Mercer in Dark River?" he asked.

"I did, but I didn't get a chance to go in and file a report. Before I could do that, I got a call from Veronica, and she told me about that anonymous tip she'd gotten about you."

Nick cursed again. The timing for that couldn't be a coincidence.

"Veronica was shaken up and asked me to come over right away. She lives on the outskirts of Lubbock so I hurried there." Hallie stopped, squeezed her eyes shut a moment and shook her head.

"What happened when you got to her house?" he pressed when she didn't continue.

Hallie stooped down and ran her index finger gently over David's cheek. She kept her attention on the boy while she spoke. "Veronica wasn't there. There were no signs of a struggle or a break-in. She was just gone."

Her voice broke on the last word. "If I'd called the Lubbock cops before I left my place, that might not have happened."

Maybe. But it was just as possible that whoever had Veronica had taken her within minutes or even seconds of the woman phoning Hallie.

Nick stooped down, too, meeting Hallie at eye level. "The Lubbock cops know Veronica's missing?"

Her nod was shaky, and Nick could practically feel the guilt coming off her in hot, thick waves. Guilt that wouldn't do any good.

He stood, taking out his phone. "I'll call Lubbock PD and see if they have any updates."

Maybe, just maybe, they'd found the woman. Ditto for Leigh finding the person who'd broken into Hallie's house.

"I'm not giving David back to social services," Hallie insisted. "I believe he's in danger, and I can better protect him than whoever they give him to."

Nick didn't dispute that last part, but he couldn't withhold information regarding the baby's whereabouts. Still, maybe the cops wouldn't give Hallie a hassle since she had the paperwork to transfer the custody.

His phone rang before he could press the number for the police station, and Nick frowned when he saw the name on the screen.

"It's Steve Fain," he told Hallie.

Nick hadn't planned on talking to Steve tonight, but he welcomed a conversation. And he especially wanted to know why Steve had thought there'd been a cover-up with the baby market bust.

"Is Hallie with you?" Steve demanded the moment Nick answered.

Nick took a second to consider how to answer that, and giving Hallie a sign to be quiet, he put the call on speaker. "Why do you ask?"

Steve belted out some profanity. "Is she with you or not?" he snapped.

"No." Nick didn't mind the lie, either. He wanted to know what he was up against before he shared Hallie and David's location with anyone.

"She'll probably come to you then because I don't know who else she can turn to." Steve said it like gospel. "When she does, you'll need to take her into custody right away."

The shock, and yeah, the outrage tightened Hallie's face. She had to tighten her mouth, no doubt to stop herself from blurting out something to Steve.

"And why would I need to do that?" Nick asked, keeping his tone like a casual shrug.

Steve didn't hesitate. "Because the cops are looking for her in connection with a woman's death. Nick, they believe Hallie murdered someone."

Chapter Two

Everything inside Hallie went still. For a couple of seconds anyway. The cops believed she'd murdered someone? Why would they think that? Better yet, who did they suspect her of killing?

An answer immediately came to her. One that sent her heart pounding.

"Veronica," she whispered on a rise of breath, and she would have blurted out more if Nick hadn't motioned again for her to stay silent.

She clamped her teeth over her bottom lip and glanced down at David when he squirmed. He was too young to understand what was going on, but it was possible he was picking up on the tension. Hoping to soothe him, she ran her hand over his arm and tried to level her breathing.

"The Lubbock cops are looking for Hallie?" Nick asked Steve.

"That's what I've heard. They want to question her about the death of a woman named Kelsey Marris."

Nick's eyebrow was raised when he looked over at her. He was no doubt wanting to know who that was.

But Hallie had to shake her head. She'd never heard the name before, and she had no idea why Steve or anyone else had connected this woman to her. Especially why they'd connected her to killing someone she didn't even know.

"Who is she," Nick asked Steve, "and why do the cops believe Hallie would have anything to do with her death?"

"Her *murder,*" Steve said, emphasizing the word. "From what I've been able to gather, Kelsey is the biological mother of the baby Hallie is trying to adopt."

This time, there was no stillness inside her. The emotions whipped through her like an F-5 tornado. Hallie couldn't shake her head fast enough, and it took every ounce of willpower she had not to demand that Steve admit he was lying.

Mercy, she needed it to be a lie.

This Kelsey Marris wasn't David's mother. She couldn't be. The ATF and the FBI had run an exhaustive search after David had been found with the militia. So had she. And no one had been able to find his parents.

Because there'd been no match.

That reminder slammed her with another round of emotions and thoughts. Sick, gut-tightening thoughts. After all, someone had given birth to him. David had a father and a mother. And the only reason the match hadn't existed was because neither of his biological parents had done something to put them in one of the many databases that existed.

"There's proof this Kelsey Marris gave birth to the boy?" Nick pressed Steve.

"I haven't personally seen the evidence, but I've been told it exists. And no, I'm not going to tell you my source. I'm a PI now, and if I betray a trust, it could cause me to lose clients."

Nick cursed. "If what you've said is true, Hallie is facing a hell of a lot worse than losing some clients. How did this all come about? How did the Lubbock cops connect Hallie to Kelsey?"

"I don't know," Steve said, and he repeated it in a much louder voice. "I'm only getting bits and pieces, but I wanted to give you a heads-up. Because I know Hallie and you were once close. I figured you could convince her that it's in her best interest to go ahead and talk to the cops."

Steve used the word *close* in the same tone as someone would say *lovers*. Nick and she hadn't been. Heck, they'd never even kissed, but Hallie had heard the rumors about Nick and her breaking the rules and having an affair. Rumors that she suspected started because there had been a strong sexual attraction between them.

And it was still there.

It didn't seem to matter that she didn't want it. The heat had a mind of its own.

"If it's in her best interest," she heard Nick repeat to Steve. There was plenty of disdain in his tone. "Her best interest would be for this asinine accusation to have never happened because I know Hallie didn't kill anyone. I'd bet my life on it," he insisted.

Hallie welcomed the support, and it got her mentally back on track. A track that had nothing to do with rumors about Nick and her.

"I plan on making some calls to find out what's hearsay and fact," Nick added a moment later.

"Good. You should do that," Steve agreed. "But just don't let your personal feelings for her get in the way of doing what you need to do. It's your duty to have her go to the cops."

She saw the muscles tighten and flex in Nick's jaw. Saw, too, the anger spurt to the surface. Hallie agreed with the anger and had plenty of her own. What Steve had just said was insulting.

"From what I've heard, you've been telling people there was a cover-up with the militia raid." Nick tossed the words out there. "Any truth to that?"

Silence from Steve. Silence that lasted several long moments. "So, I guess you've been talking to Hallie."

Nick went silent for a while, too, and clearly dodged Steve's comment when he fired back, "Why would you think there was a cover-up?"

"It was just the way things went down," Steve answered on a huff. "You know, with those babies being there. We had a man who had inside contact with the militia, somebody who should have reported the babies to us. To you," Steve said with emphasis.

There had indeed been someone on the inside. On

two different occasions, agents had visited the militia under the guise of wanting to join so they could establish themselves as moles. When those attempts had failed, the ATF had turned to a criminal informant, Darius Lawler, who was already a member.

To the best of Hallie's knowledge, Darius had never said a thing about a black market baby operation. The militia compound had been large, over fifty acres with more than a dozen buildings, so maybe he simply hadn't known about it. However, no one in the ATF had been able to question Darius because he'd disappeared the night of the raid.

Hallie hadn't given Darius much thought after that night. She'd first been healing from the gunshot wound and then rethinking her future. After coming so close to dying, she hadn't wanted the badge. Not any longer.

But she had wanted David.

And that's why she'd started her certification with social services the day she'd gotten out of the hospital. She'd loved him from the first moment she'd laid eyes on him. In fact, she hadn't thought she could possibly love him more than she had in that moment, but she'd been wrong. She got a reminder of that every time she looked at him.

"Next time you want to accuse me of something," Nick snarled, "do it to my face. Don't go behind my back and stir up gossip."

Nick hit the end call button and then pressed "decline" when Steve tried to call him right back.

"You really didn't know anything about this Kelsey Marris?" Nick asked while he did a search for the woman on his phone.

"Nothing, and I won't believe she was David's mother unless I see proof." Then, something else occurred to her. "Have you seen any recent info about David? Anyone making inquiries about him? Anyone asking questions about the adoption?"

"Nothing," he echoed. "But I don't like all the things that are happening right now. Steve asking about a cover-up. Veronica missing. The break-in at your house. The cops wanting to question you about a murdered woman." He stopped and scanned what popped up on his screen. It was a picture, and Nick turned his phone so she could see it. "That's Kelsey," he said.

Hallie went closer, her attention fixed to the grainy photo. *Young.* That was her first impression. Kelsey looked like a teenager. An attractive one with light brown hair and pale gray eyes.

Hallie tried to pick through the woman's features and find any resemblance to David, but she didn't see it at all. But maybe that's because she didn't want to. She didn't want this murdered woman to have given birth to him. Or, for that matter, to have any connection whatsoever to him.

"Kelsey had her twenty-first birthday about a month ago," Nick explained. "At the time of her death, she was working as a waitress at a mom-and-pop burger place and was sharing an apartment with two other roommates."

So, Kelsey didn't appear to be swimming in money. Maybe that meant if she was indeed David's mother that she hadn't sold him to the militia. Perhaps the militia had kidnapped him, and for whatever reason, Kelsey hadn't reported it.

"This isn't a mug shot," Hallie muttered.

"No. But she does have a juvie record for shoplifting, false ID and underage drinking. This is a photo one of her friends gave to the cops when Kelsey went missing. The friend is Ty Levine." Nick pulled up his picture as well and showed it to her.

Also young with dark hair and brown eyes. Seeing those particular features gave Hallie a punch of dread. Because David also had dark hair. Of course, plenty of babies did. It could mean nothing.

But it felt like something.

"I've never heard Ty Levine's name come up, either, and I don't recognize him," Hallie said. "Neither Kelsey nor he was in any of the reports of the searches for David's relatives."

Nick made a sound of agreement. Followed by a sound of frustration. He scrubbed his hand over his face before he pulled up another photo. One also from social media, and it appeared to have been taken at a party. In it, Ty was sporting a cocky grin, and he had his arm slung around Kelsey's shoulders. Kelsey's smile was shy. Her eyes tipped up to Ty. It was the look of a girl in love.

"I think my first phone call should be to Leigh," Nick told her, jarring her out of her thoughts about the couple in the picture.

Hallie certainly wasn't on a first name basis with Sheriff Leigh Mercer, but since she was about to be Nick's sister-in-law, he obviously was. Maybe that meant he'd be able to get more from her than the Lubbock cops. Of course, Nick would have to talk to them, too. So would Hallie.

But there could be a huge problem with that.

What if the cops didn't believe she'd had nothing to do with Kelsey's death and then took her into custody? With Veronica missing, where would that leave David? They'd likely call in another foster parent. One who might not be able to protect him if that intruder returned.

Hallie took hold of Nick's hand before he could press in Leigh's number. "You've got to promise me that if something goes wrong, you'll keep David safe." She got right in his face. "Swear it."

Nick didn't back away from her and didn't tell her to tone it down a whole bunch of notches. He stared at her and then nodded. "I swear I'll keep him safe."

She released the breath she'd been holding and nearly went limp with relief. Nick was as good as his word. That's why Hallie had believed him when he'd told her he hadn't had any part in the chaos and confusion that was going on now. He had told the truth then, and he'd told it now. If it came down to it, he would take care of the child that she already thought of as her son.

Nick kept his attention on her. Their eyes stayed locked. And she wanted to groan when she felt the stir of heat again.

Really?

Now wasn't the time for this. Maybe it never would be. But at least she didn't have to continue to stand there, staring and lusting. That's because David whimpered again, and Hallie hurried to him. She sat down on the floor next to the baby and gently rocked his carrier.

"I'm calling Leigh now," he said while he continued to give Hallie a long, lingering look.

Perhaps she hadn't been the only one to feel the attraction. But if so, he had pushed it away and made the call. Like the one with Steve, he also put this one on speaker, and within seconds, Hallie heard the sheriff answer.

"What's wrong?" Leigh immediately asked. Obviously, she wasn't accustomed to getting late night calls from her fiancé's brother.

Nick didn't answer the sheriff but instead went with a question of his own. "In the past couple of hours, has anyone gotten in touch with you about Hallie?"

"Since I doubt you have ESP, it sounds like someone has indeed been in touch with *you* about her. If it's Hallie herself, I need to talk to her. Just a couple of hours ago, she reported she'd had a break-in at her house. I sent out a deputy to have a look around, but she wasn't there. He said there didn't appear to be any signs of a struggle though the front door was wide open. The three calls I've made to her all went straight to voice mail."

That's because after she'd learned that Veronica was missing, Hallie had turned off her phone and tossed it so that it couldn't be triangulated and used to track her. In case the intruder was still after David and her, she hadn't wanted to make it easy for him to find her. Anyone who could jam her security system wouldn't have had any trouble tracing a regular cell phone.

"You've been trying to call her about the break-in?" Nick asked.

The sheriff sighed loud enough for Hallie to hear it over the phone. "That, and Lubbock PD wants to question her about the death of Kelsey Marris."

Hallie made a silent groan. So, it was true. Steve hadn't misspoke.

"Death or murder?" Nick challenged.

"Right now, it's being called a suspicious death. She overdosed, but her friend—a guy named Ty Levine—is claiming she was murdered, that she didn't use drugs. Some of her other friends also confirmed that they'd never seen her use." Leigh paused. "Why? You know something about it?"

"To be determined. I'll get back to you if I hear anything. For now though, do you have anything on the intruder who broke into Hallie's house?"

"I had a deputy canvass the area, but no one saw anything suspicious. It'd help a lot if Hallie came in and made a report, and then I'd have specific details like a time and description of the perp that I could use to re-canvass the neighborhood."

Hallie could give the time of the break-in, but she was short of any useful info about the intruder. She'd seen none of his features, but that was still something she'd need to tell the sheriff. Any and all details mattered in an investigation like this.

Unfortunately, if she went into the Dark River Sheriff's Office, Sheriff Mercer might be forced to take her into custody. Before that could happen, Hallie wanted to find answers. Answers as to who was behind this and why they were creating this nightmare.

"Have you gotten any reports on a missing foster mother, Veronica Richards?" Nick asked the sheriff a moment later.

"No. Why? Is she connected to the break-in or the dead woman in Lubbock?"

"Sorry, but again that's to be determined. I'll make sure you're in the info loop when I find out anything." Nick added a "thanks" before he ended the call, and his attention went back to Hallie. "You ditched your phone? Is that why Leigh hasn't been able to get in touch with you?"

She nodded. "I bought a burner at a gas station."

Nick nodded as well, but the deep breath he took was more of a weary sigh. "I know you don't want to hear this, but you're going to need to speak to Lubbock PD. I'll take you." He quickly added before she could voice the concern that had to be all over her face, "And if it turns out that you need a lawyer, I've got some I can call for you."

The panic came. Mercy, did it, and it leaped all the way to her throat. "I didn't kill Kelsey Marris."

"I know you didn't." Nick said it as if he had no doubts about that. "But the longer you wait to talk to the cops, the worse it looks for you. How solid is your paperwork for David? By that I mean did Veronica cut any corners by allowing you to take him tonight?"

"It's all legit. Veronica gave me signed permission, and I have all the adoption and custody documents." But then she groaned when she realized where all of that was. "They're at my house."

"Okay. Then, we'll need to go by there first and get them. I don't want anyone questioning your right to have David."

Neither did she, but Hallie had plenty of other concerns. "It might not be safe to go to my place."

"We'll have to make it safe," he said just as fast. "Where are you parked? I didn't see a vehicle when I got home."

"I left my car on the street behind your house." Hallie had done that so she could go in through Nick's backyard where she was less likely to be seen by one of his neighbors.

"You can leave it there. We'll take my SUV. It's reinforced with bullet resistant sides and windows. I'll also call Leigh back and arrange for her or one of her deputies to meet us at your place."

She was about to remind him that could be a problem, too, because Leigh might insist on taking her statement about the break-in. However, Hallie didn't even have a chance to spell out her concerns because the slash of lights stopped her cold.

Headlights turning into the driveway of Nick's house.

"I guess you're not expecting company," she muttered.

"No," he said, already heading to the front window. He peered out.

Then, he cursed.

"Get down," Nick warned her.

And he drew his gun.

Chapter Three

Nick kept his eyes on the truck that stopped in front of his house and braced himself for the worst.

With everything he'd just learned, he had no doubts there was trouble brewing. Trouble that likely went back to the militia bust six months ago. And now a woman was dead, another was missing. Added to that, Nick was a 1000 percent sure that Hallie and that precious little boy were in danger.

Hell.

David had already been through way too much in his young life. He'd essentially been caught in the middle of a raid that'd injured several agents and militia members. Bullets had flown that night, and it was a miracle that David and the rest of the babies hadn't been hurt.

"Is it Steve?" Hallie asked.

That was a good guess. It'd been Nick's guess as well, especially after the phone conversation he'd had with the former agent. But it wasn't Steve who stepped out of the vehicle. Steve was tall and lanky, and this guy had a much bulkier build.

Because their visitor kept the truck running with the headlights on, Nick got a good look at the guy as he made his way to the house. And he was someone Nick was pretty sure he recognized, thanks to a photo he'd seen just this very night.

"It's Ty Levine," he relayed to Hallie, and he got the reaction that he'd expected from her. A sound of surprise mixed with a huge amount of concern.

Nick was plenty concerned, too, especially considering Kelsey's suspicious death. He still wasn't sure what Ty had been to Kelsey and vice versa, but the picture of the two sure made it seem as if they'd been lovers. Nick needed to find out if that was true. Heck, he needed to find out plenty of things, but Nick had to debate just how big of a risk it was to try to get those answers from Ty right now. He cut the debate short though when the man stepped onto the porch.

"Stay down," Nick instructed Hallie. Whether she would or not was anyone's guess, but he was hoping she'd put David first, and that meant staying close to the baby and away from their visitor.

Ty didn't knock, and Nick watched as the man took out a folded piece of paper that he first tried to tuck in the door. When that didn't work, he laid it on the welcome mat. What he didn't do was walk away. Ty stared down at the paper as if he, too, was having a debate as to what to do next. Nick ended that for him by unlocking and opening the door. Not wide. He only opened it a fraction and glared out at the man.

"Oh," Ty said, clearly startled. His eyes were already wide but went even wider when his attention landed on Nick's gun. He dropped back a step. "You're Agent Nick Brodie?"

"I am. What do you want?" Nick snapped, making sure he sounded like the lawman he was.

Ty swallowed hard. "I'm Ty Levine, and I wasn't trespassing or anything," he blurted out. "I was just leaving you a note to tell you to call me because I think we need to talk."

There was no "I think" to it. They did indeed need to talk, but Nick took some precautions first. He made a quick check over his shoulder to make sure Hallie was hidden. She was. Nick kept himself angled in the doorway so that Ty wouldn't be able to see her.

Nick also did a visual search of the man to make sure he wasn't armed. Ty didn't appear to be, and his tight jeans and muscle shirt didn't conceal much. However, he could be using a slide holster like Hallie.

Ty reached down, picked up the note and handed it to Nick. "Kelsey's dead," he said. His voice cracked, and he turned away, staring out into the side yard. Too bad about that because Nick would have preferred to look the man in the eyes.

"Keep your hands where I can see them," Nick warned him, and he took a quick look at the note. It was short and to the point. "I need to talk to you about Kelsey Marris." Ty had included his phone number.

"Why come to me about Kelsey?" Nick asked. "Lubbock PD is handling that investigation. In fact, why come to me at all?"

Ty swallowed hard and dropped back another step. If he kept that up, he'd fall backward off the porch steps. Of course, these nerves could all be an act, something that Nick made sure to remember.

"Yeah, the Lubbock cops are looking into it," Ty replied several moments later, "but I got this call saying you were in on that. That you knew about some of the stuff going on."

Damn it. Who was doing this? Steve, maybe? Maybe someone just trying to stir up trouble. Well, the stirring was working.

Nick had to tamp down his temper before he could ask, "You got a call about me?"

Ty nodded. "The guy didn't say who he was, but he told me you knew what'd happened to Kelsey." His gaze finally came back to Nick. "What did happen to her?"

"I don't know," Nick answered honestly. "Did this caller say anything else?"

The man took a moment as if considering that. "No. Not really. Just that I was to talk to you if I wanted to know what'd happened." When he paused again, his chin came up. "She didn't kill herself with drugs. I don't want you or anybody else thinking that. Her momma overdosed when she was a kid, and it made Kelsey swear off ever using them."

That didn't mean Kelsey hadn't, but Nick was leaning toward this not having anything to do with drugs.

"You were in love with Kelsey?" Nick asked. He softened his tone a notch.

Ty shrugged. "I cared about her."

Which meant no, he hadn't been in love with her. "You were lovers?"

"Yeah. We were together for a while. Until she moved over to Ransom Ridge to work there." He paused again. "I know she had a kid. The guy who called me told me that."

"The same guy who said I'd know what happened to Kelsey?" Nick asked.

"Same one," Ty stated. "He said Kelsey had had a kid and that you knew about it."

Nick didn't bother denying that the first he'd heard of Kelsey had been less than a half hour ago. And he had no proof whatsoever that she'd had a child.

"I didn't know Kelsey got pregnant," Ty went on. "I swear, she never told me anything like that." He made another of those long glances into the yard. "I guess it's possible the kid is mine though."

Yes, it was possible, but again Nick would need DNA proof. Considering Ty's visit and other speculation was being orchestrated by someone making anonymous calls, it was possible David's paternity had nothing whatsoever to do with Kelsey or Ty. This might be some kind of attempt to smear Nick's name. Or smear what'd happened with the militia raid.

"If Kelsey had given birth to a child, would she have voluntarily given it up?" Nick asked.

Another shrug from Ty. "Maybe. Don't know why she wouldn't have told me though. Well, if it was mine. If it wasn't, then that'd explain why she moved off. She mighta thought I'd be mad because she'd cheated on me." He paused again, his jaw hardening. "And yeah, I woulda been mad."

Nick latched right on to that. "Did you and Kelsey have run-ins?" He thought that was a better way of asking the man if there'd ever been any physical violence. Not that Nick was sure what that would tell him, but right now, he didn't know what pieces of this puzzle were important to figuring out what was going on.

"I guess you could call it run-ins. We didn't always see eye to eye." But then, Ty's own eyes widened. "I didn't hit her or anything if that's what you're asking. And I wouldn't have hit her if she'd cheated on me, either," he snarled. "I would have just left and let her get on with her life." Ty swallowed hard. "But she didn't get on with it. She died."

Yeah, and Nick really needed to know the reason that'd happened. "Did Kelsey have any connections to anyone in a militia?" Nick asked. "Or maybe a connection to anyone who was doing something illegal?"

Ty squared his shoulders. "Are you accusing me of something?"

Nick hadn't been, but Ty's reaction brought out Nick's lawman's instincts. Something was here. Maybe Ty's own connection to the militia.

"The Brothers of Freedom," Nick said, referring to

the name of the militia that had run the black market baby ring. "What do you know about them?"

"Nothing," Ty snapped, "and I gotta go." He obviously meant it, too. The man barreled down the porch steps and hurried back to his truck.

Nick considered going after him, but he didn't want to leave Hallie alone. Especially since he had a really bad feeling about the way all of this was going down.

Ty's visit had spurred a lot of suspicion, and Nick wanted to look past the good ole boy demeanor and figure out if this meeting had been orchestrated for some reason other than Ty and that anonymous call.

It was possible that everything Ty had just told him was a lie.

Including that he'd had no knowledge before tonight that Kelsey had been pregnant. Of course, it was entirely possible that the woman hadn't been. Speculation that she'd had a child and that the child was David was just that—speculation.

"I heard," Hallie immediately said the moment Nick stepped back into the house. "You think Ty had some part in the militia?"

"I'm about to find out."

He locked up and did something he rarely did. He set the security system and motioned for her to bring David to his office that was just up the hall. Nick considered suggesting that she go ahead and take the baby to the guest room so she could get some rest. But he seriously doubted there'd be much resting tonight. Plus he didn't want them out of his sight just yet. Not until he knew a little more about what was going on.

With the baby still sleeping, she brought him into the office and set the carrier on the floor while Nick went to his desk and booted up his laptop. He opened the file he'd created for the militia investigation. It didn't include all the info though. Some of the reports were classified to protect the two agents who'd tried to infiltrate the militia. No need to spread their names around because the pair might have to repeat an attempt to get inside other militia groups.

But Hallie's and Nick's names had hit the media.

Nick wasn't positive of the source for that, but he suspected it was someone at the hospital. Hallie and he had both been shot, had both required immediate medical attention. That meant a lot of people had come in contact with them when they'd been trying to save their lives. Leaks happened, and if there were any members of the Brothers of Freedom still around who might want to get revenge at having their operation torn apart, then those members could be causing all this trouble.

And that's the direction Nick was leaning right now.

There was no way to know if the ATF had gotten all the people involved in the militia, and it only took one to put a plan into action to get back at anyone who'd had a part in the bust. That *anyone* would definitely include Hallie and him.

With Hallie right by his side and her attention on the computer screen, Nick typed in Ty's name to do a search of the law enforcement databases. Nothing came up. He tried variations of the spelling and did a side search to see if the man had ever used a known alias. Still nothing.

"Maybe Ty has a family member or friends who were militia members," she suggested. "I could try to dig around and see if there's a connection."

Hallie had been good at doing exactly that when she had worked for him, but it was yet something else that would have to go on the back burner. Ty might have a big part in what'd happened to Hallie, Kelsey and even Veronica, but right now it was best for them to deal with the problem of Lubbock PD needing to question Hallie. With all the anonymous calls going around, Nick didn't want cops showing up at his door to take her into custody.

He turned to her, figuring that she already knew what he was going to say because he saw the dread in her eyes. "I have a contact in Lubbock PD," he said. "Detective Miriam Gable. She's solid."

Hallie stayed quiet a moment, her gaze sliding to David before meeting Nick's again. "I remember you dated her for a while."

Nick shouldn't have been surprised that Hallie would have remembered that. He hadn't exactly kept the dating a secret, and there was always gossip about that sort of thing. Heck, there'd been gossip about Hallie and him. Probably because of the heated looks they'd often given each other.

Like now.

Yeah, it was heated all right, and it caused him to curse again. He really didn't want this to get in the way. Not with everything they had to do. But Nick could already tell that it was going to be a problem.

"Things ended well," he assured her. "She won't make an interview hard for you because of me."

Again, Hallie paused and then she nodded. The nod was his greenlight to take out his phone, scroll through his contacts and call Miriam. Because of the late hour, Nick was ready to leave her a message, but Miriam answered on the second ring.

"Please tell me you're calling about Hallie Stanton," Miriam greeted.

Nick barely bit back a groan. "Please don't tell me you got an anonymous call about me."

"I did, and the caller said you'd know how to get in touch with Hallie. True or false?" Miriam asked in her no-nonsense tone. Actually, she was no-nonsense in general, which was why they'd hit it off. Nick was still trying to suss out why the hitting it off had ground to a halt.

"True," Nick admitted. "She came to me after someone broke into her home. I want to bring her in for an interview. *An interview*," Nick stated. "Hallie's a former special agent with the ATF. She wouldn't kill a woman, especially one she didn't even know."

"You're talking about Kelsey Marris. Yes, I need to *interview* her about that, and I'd prefer this not wait until morning. I need you to go ahead and bring her to the police station."

"I will. We have a stop to make first." They needed to get those papers about David from her house. "But we should be there in about an hour. I'm hoping you'll also be able to fill me in on the search for Veronica Richards."

"Veronica Richards," Miriam repeated. "You haven't heard?"

Hell. That bad feeling in his gut went up a notch. "Heard what?"

"We found her." Miriam's response was fast and flat.

Even though he hadn't put this call on speaker, Hallie was close enough that she obviously heard. She made a sharp sound of relief.

"Is she okay?" Hallie blurted out.

Miriam certainly didn't give a quick answer this time. "Hallie?" she finally questioned. "Is that you?"

"Yes," Hallie replied. "Is Veronica okay?"

Again, Miriam hesitated. "Not really. We'll talk about that when you get to the station. I need you to come in *now*."

Chapter Four

A feeling of sick dread washed over Hallie in thick waves, and she pressed her hand against the wall to try to steady herself. It didn't help. Nothing would at this point, and she wasn't sure she could steel herself up enough to hear whatever else Miriam had to say.

"Is Veronica alive?" Hallie managed to ask once she'd gathered enough breath to speak.

"She is," Miriam said after another of those heart-stopping pauses.

Hallie wanted to latch on to that. *She was alive.* However, there was that edge in Miriam's voice. The edge that told Hallie that yes, Veronica hadn't been killed, but there was some bad news to go along with that.

"Like I said," Miriam continued a moment later, "come in for the interview, and I can give you an update on Veronica."

Nick groaned. So did Hallie. Because this sounded like emotional blackmail.

"Look, I'll bring Hallie to the police station but tell us Veronica's condition now," Nick demanded.

"All right," Miriam said after a sigh that managed to sound annoyed. "A little less than an hour ago, Veronica was found unconscious by the side of the road about a quarter of a mile from her house. She has a head injury. Just how bad that injury is, I don't know because I'm waiting on a call from the hospital."

Hallie figured a head injury could mean anything from a concussion to brain damage. Mercy, she hoped it wasn't the latter and that Veronica would be able to recover from this. Better yet, Hallie prayed she'd not only recover but would also be able to tell them exactly who'd done this to her.

"Has Veronica regained consciousness?" Nick asked.

"Not as of ten minutes ago, she hadn't. That's when I got the last update from the deputy I have with her," Miriam answered. "When she does wake up, I'll go to the hospital and question her."

"I need to see her, too," Hallie insisted.

"No." There wasn't even a moment's hesitation that time from Miriam. "Not until I've talked with her and not until her doctor says it's okay for her to have visitors. I'll add one more condition. You won't be seeing Veronica at all until after you finish your interview with me. Veronica's alive, but another woman isn't. I need answers about that."

So did Hallie. She desperately had to find out what was going on so that David or anyone else, Nick included, wouldn't be in danger. That meant cooperating with Miriam and praying that the cop didn't arrest her on the spot.

"Hallie will also need to talk to the Dark River sheriff about the break-in at her house," Nick informed Miriam. "But you get first dibs." He checked his watch. "We have that one stop to make first at Hallie's house, and then I'll get her to the police station."

He ended the call, maybe because he thought Miriam might object to the "one stop." But it was a necessary one in case any questions came up about why Hallie had David with her. Those papers could prevent him from being taken from her. Well, hopefully they would.

"What if Miriam arrests me and then won't let you take temporary custody of David?" Hallie muttered.

Nick's gaze met hers, and he must have seen that this particular fear was tearing her apart because he sighed. Then, he slipped his arm around her and pulled her to him.

"I have friends in Child Protective Services, and I'll convince whoever needs convincing that it's too dangerous to place David with another foster parent," he told her. "That's not a lie. It wouldn't be safe for him or another family."

Hallie hung on to each word. Just as she hung on to Nick. She hated having to rely on him like this, but she'd do anything to make sure no one harmed her little boy. Anything, too, to hold on to her sanity, and right now, Nick was helping her with that as well.

Nick eased back, reexamining her expression for a

couple of long moments before he finally pulled himself away from her. "Let's get this interview done so you can get some rest. Then, we can focus on talking to Veronica and then Leigh." He tipped his head toward David. "I'm guessing the base for his car seat is in your vehicle?"

"It is." And that reminder brought on a fresh round of fear.

When she'd parked and walked to Nick's house, she'd been mainly concerned with finding out if he'd had any possible involvement in the break-in at her house. But now her concern was taking David back outside.

"All right. Give me your keys, and I'll park your car in my garage and install the base for the infant seat into my SUV," Nick explained, easing some of that fear. "We can load David in and won't open the garage door until we're leaving."

Hallie fished out the keys from her pocket and handed them to him. "Thank you. It's a blue Honda Accord. It's parked just on the other side of your neighbor's house." Since neither Nick nor the neighbor had fences, it wouldn't take him long to get there.

He nodded and headed for the back door. "I'll lock up when I leave and reset the security system," Nick explained. "I'll open the garage with my phone and will come back through there." He motioned to the side door. "I'll have to disengage the security when I come in again, so stay right here with David until I've given you the okay."

Hallie would indeed stay inside. She didn't want to do anything that would put David in harm's way.

"Be careful," she told him, meeting his eyes one last time before he used his phone to disarm the security system so he could go out without triggering the alarm. He closed the door behind him, and she watched from the kitchen window as he darted off the porch and disappeared into the night.

Trying to tamp down the tightness in her chest and stomach, she went back to kneel by David, and she waited. And waited. Hallie was certain that time didn't actually come to a stop, but it certainly seemed as if it had.

Each second dragged by, and with each of those seconds came the bad thoughts and possibilities. Thoughts that the masked intruder would ambush Nick in the darkness and then come after David again. She quickly countered that one though with the reminder that Nick was armed and knew how to take care of himself. Plus he'd be vigilant.

Of course, vigilance hadn't stopped either of them from being shot during the militia raid.

She touched the scars on her stomach. The bullets had entered there and done plenty of damage. She was minus one kidney and would never be able to give birth to a child because her injuries had forced her to have a hysterectomy. Once Nick learned that, he might think it was the reason she'd latched so hard on to David, but it was much more than that. Right from the start, she'd felt as if he were already hers.

Hallie hoped that legally he soon would be.

She couldn't lose him, and she prayed that Veronica would be able to help them put a stop to any possibility of that happening. Veronica could maybe help the cops ID and arrest the person responsible for the attack. Once he or she was behind bars, then Hallie would be able to live out her life in peace with David. Veronica might have some peace, too.

While more of those long seconds ticked off, the image of Nick flashed into Hallie's mind. Images no doubt brought on because of the way he'd so easily pulled her into his arms. Because of the way her body had so easily reacted to the gesture. And to him.

Before the militia raid, she'd had plenty of fantasies about Nick. Kissing him. Making love with him. Maybe even having more than that. Of course, it could have never happened as long as he was her boss, and afterward, after the shooting, well, she hadn't been able to think of anything like kissing or making love.

Unfortunately, she thought of it all now.

With Nick.

This strong attraction that she felt for him was not amplified by the stress and nerves, she assured herself. The tingling in her body would go away as soon as she was able to put some space between Nick and her. But for now the heat continued to be relentless.

Until Hallie heard the grinding sound of the garage door opening and then closing.

A fresh wave of fear and worry came because she knew it could be an intruder. Maybe the same one who'd broken into her place earlier. Staying on the side of the fridge so that her body would act as a shield for David, Hallie drew her gun and waited some more. She didn't have to wait long though this time.

"It's me," Nick announced, coming in through the side door that led to the garage. She heard the door close behind him, and he came into the kitchen.

Instant relief flooded her, and she stood again to re-holster her Glock. "Did you see anyone?" she asked.

He shook his head. "I saw a remote opener on your driver's side visor. I'm guessing that means you have a garage at your house? Good," Nick said when she nodded. "Because we'll use it." He paused. "I also called Leigh while I was driving your car over, and she said she can meet us at your place in about thirty minutes."

Hallie didn't have any objections to that. "All right," she agreed.

It would be good to have the backup in case something went wrong. Also, maybe while the sheriff was there, she could have a look through the house and take anything the intruder had left behind. If one of Leigh's deputies hadn't already done it, that was.

Hallie didn't believe the CSIs had been called in yet, and they perhaps wouldn't be. Small towns like Dark River didn't always have the budget to do such things unless there was a crime with injuries. Of course, she had stopped the intruder before any injuries could happen, but she figured he'd planned to hurt or even kill her so he could take David. And that's why Hallie would press Leigh for the CSIs to do a thorough sweep of the place. They might be able to find something they could use to ID the man.

"I spoke to my boss," Nick explained. "I told him I had something personal come up, and he gave me some time off. No questions asked. But I will need to fill him in soon."

She nodded. That soon would no doubt have to be today after this meeting with Miriam.

"Steve called me again," Nick added a moment later. That definitely got her attention. "I didn't answer, but it's obvious he intends to keep trying to talk to us. He could have your house staked out. If so, Leigh can help us get rid of him since it's her jurisdiction."

Mercy, she hadn't even considered Steve being at her house. She didn't have the energy or the time to deal with him tonight, and if Leigh could step in and deal with that, then Hallie was all for it.

"I'll help get David in the car," Nick offered, and he reached down for the baby's car seat.

However, his hand froze when they heard the sound of the garage door opening again. Hallie was sure there was a whole lot more than just alarm in her eyes when her gaze slashed to Nick's. There had to be some terror, too, since that's exactly what she was feeling.

"I didn't open it," he said, moving in front of her and drawing his gun. "Someone's out there."

NICK WANTED TO believe the garage door had malfunctioned or that he'd accidentally hit the app on his phone to open it. But he seriously doubted it was either of those things. Considering what had already happened tonight with Hallie, this was almost certainly an intruder.

One who might want to finish what he'd started at Hallie's house.

"How would someone open the garage door?" Hallie muttered, but she immediately waved off that question. Because she no doubt already knew the answer. She'd gotten into his house, and someone else could do the same. In fact, it was probably a heck of a lot easier to jimmy a garage door than to pick a lock.

"Get down," Nick told Hallie.

Thankfully, she was already doing just that, and moving fast, she positioned herself in front of David. She also drew her gun. He knew she'd use it if necessary, but Nick didn't want it to come down to that. Because if it did, it'd mean things had gone from bad to worse. It would also mean the baby would be in the middle of the gunfire.

"Call 911," Nick whispered to her. "Report a break-in. I want sirens blaring ASAP."

That would likely get the intruder running, which would set up a good news/bad news scenario. Nick wanted to confront this SOB and find out what the hell was going on. But he didn't want that at Hallie and David's expense. He'd rather have the intruder hightail it out of there so he could then deal with him another time, another place.

Nick moved away from Hallie and David and listened while Hallie made the 911 call. Listened, too, for any sounds of footsteps or movement both in the garage and the house. He didn't hear anything, but he took up position on the side of the mudroom door. Because if the intruder entered the house through the garage, then he'd have to come this way.

And Nick waited.

He peered around the doorjamb, paying close attention to the knob on the door that led from the garage. By keeping to the side, he wouldn't be in a direct line of fire if the snake just threw open the door and started shooting. In this position, he could also keep watch on both the front and back of the house in case the intruder was using the garage as a decoy and distraction.

Which Nick figured was a strong possibility.

Unless this guy was truly an idiot, he would have known that Hallie and he would have heard the garage door opening. It would have been quieter to slip through a window, especially since the security system was off for the couple of seconds that it'd taken Nick to get back into his house after moving Hallie's car into the garage. And maybe the intruder had done exactly that.

Which caused a knot to tighten his gut.

Because it meant there could be two of them. One

attacker was plenty bad enough considering how high the stakes were right now, but two could come at him from both the garage and another part of the house.

"The cops are on their way." Hallie relayed the information when she finished the 911 call.

Since Nick lived in the city, it wouldn't take them long to get there. Maybe just a couple of minutes or less if there was already a patrol car nearby. But a lot of bad things could happen in even a short period of time.

"Keep watch on the front part of the house," he instructed.

When he gave her a quick glance, he saw that order had caused her eyes to widen. Caused more fear, too, on her face. He didn't like seeing the stark fear there, but they had to be prepared.

Nick finally heard something. Not footsteps exactly but some kind of movement in the garage. He leaned out again, taking aim at the mudroom door. Both the hinges and the lock had been reinforced, but that didn't stop the shot.

The bullet blasted through it.

Splinters burst toward him. They flew through the air and scattered across the kitchen floor around him. The sound was deafening and plenty loud enough to wake up David. The baby started crying. A very loud cry. Not good. Because it would allow the shooter to pinpoint the baby's location.

From the corner of his eye, Nick saw Hallie pull a bottle from the backpack that was on the floor next to the car seat, and the moment she put it in David's mouth, the baby's cries stopped.

But the shots didn't.

Another bullet came slamming through the mud-room door, this one tearing through more wood. And it wasn't in the same place as the first shot. This one had been aimed more in Hallie and David's direction. The SOB was actually shooting at a kid, and that caused the anger to roar through him.

Nick knew he had no choice but to return fire. He couldn't just stand there and let the baby or Hallie get hurt. He judged the shooter's location, aiming low so that the bullets wouldn't exit through the garage wall and go into his neighbor's house.

And he pulled the trigger.

Not once but twice.

His bullets ripped through the bottom part of the door, and through the now gaping holes, Nick caught sight of someone darting to the left, moving toward the front of the garage. It was just a blur of motion, and he couldn't tell if it was a man or woman, but he was betting that it was the same guy who'd attempted the earlier break-in at Hallie's.

In the distance, Nick heard another welcome sound. Sirens. And yeah, they were blaring all right just as he'd wanted. Maybe luck would be on their side, and the cops would see the shooter running from the scene. Nick wished he could do the same. See the idiot and stop him. He wanted this guy locked up for a long, long time.

"The front door," Hallie blurted out.

Nick pivoted in that direction just in time to see the doorknob jiggle as if someone was trying to jimmy the lock. Hell. Either there were indeed two of them, or the shooter from the garage hadn't run far after all.

"Come through that door and you're a dead man," Nick shouted, the anger inside him turning to rage.

The rage must have come through in his voice, too. And the guy who was turning the doorknob must have also realized that Nick wasn't bluffing. That he would indeed shoot to kill. Moments later, with the sirens growing closer, Nick heard the sound of footsteps. Not coming into the house. But running away.

"Keep down," Nick reminded Hallie.

He intended to do a quick check out the front window to try to catch a glimpse of the man who'd just tried to kill them. However, Nick stopped in his tracks when he saw the blood. And the bullet hole in the wall right next to Hallie.

That's when he realized she'd been shot.

Chapter Five

Hallie frowned at the script for the pain meds that the ER nurse tried to hand her. She had no intentions of taking anything that would dull her mind.

Or her anger.

She wanted to hang on to both right now as reminders of how close the shooter had come to hurting David. Of how close she had come to losing him tonight. The SOB was going to pay for that, and the anger—and yes, even the pain—were fueling the urgency to find the shooter now and make sure he never fired another shot at anyone.

"The bullet didn't slice very deep when it cut across your arm, but when the local anesthesia wears off, your stitches will start aching," the nurse explained.

According to her nametag, she was Connie Glover, and she'd been the one who had administered those stitches. Hallie was thankful for that. Thankful, too, that the nurse had come to the Lubbock Police Department interview room so that Nick, David and she hadn't had to go to the hospital for an exam and treatment.

Well, Hallie was partly thankful for the last one.

She wouldn't have minded going to the hospital so she could perhaps get the chance to see Veronica, but Hallie hadn't wanted to take a risk like that with David. It was best for the baby to be in the station, surrounded by cops. And it was also best for him to be sleeping. Which David was somehow managing despite the nightmarish events of the night.

To give the baby a little more room to stretch out, Hallie had moved him from his car seat and onto a makeshift bed on the interview table. Miriam had even managed to get some blankets for padding before the detective had stepped out so that Hallie and David could be examined by the nurse.

Nick had stepped out as well to try to find out if anyone had spotted the shooter, but he'd promised Hallie that he wouldn't go far. Just into the hall where he'd keep an eye on the interview room door.

It was only a precaution, he'd added.

The look he'd given her had been to try to convince her that the threat was low here. It was. Hallie was certain of that what with Nick staying so close. But any possible threat was enough to make her glad any and all precautions were being taken. It was possible there was a dirty cop or two in the building, but she seriously doubted one would go after her in here.

But why had he gone after her in the first place?

The break-in at her house had definitely been an attempt to kidnap David. Probably along with killing her, too, so there'd be no one to give a description of the kidnapper. A kidnapping like that could have been motivated by money. A ransom or a black market baby deal. So, what had changed? Why had the gunman opted to start shooting when David could have been hurt or killed?

Like her other questions, Hallie didn't have any answers. But maybe Nick or even Miriam would be able to find something to get the investigation started. Then, once she could access a computer, Hallie would start digging into Ty Levine and Kelsey Marris. Heck, into Steve as well. Even if none of them was connected to the attacks and break-in, at least she might be able to eliminate them as suspects. Right now, it felt as if everyone was a suspect, and she wasn't sure if she could trust anyone but Nick.

"I'll leave the script here in case you change your mind," the nurse said, gathering up her medical gear and dropping the prescription on the table of the interview room. She looked down at David, smiled. "Also, you'll need to see your doctor in seven days to have the stitches removed."

Seven days seemed like an eternity, but maybe, just maybe the danger would be over well before then. Hallie couldn't imagine going through another day of this level of stress much less an entire week.

She thanked the nurse, but Hallie waited until the woman was out the door before she closed her eyes for a moment and let the events of the last couple of hours wash over her. Of course, she saw images of the bullet slamming through the wall. She'd had her body over David's so he hadn't been hit with any of the flying debris. She hadn't been as lucky. Along with the bullet gashing her arm, Hallie could feel the handful of nicks on her face and neck.

The interview room door opened and Hallie whirled around, reaching for a gun that wasn't there since she'd had to surrender it when she'd entered the police station. But she soon learned a gun wasn't necessary anyway since it was Nick who came walking in.

"Did they find the shooter?" Hallie immediately asked.

Nick shook his head, a weary kind of gesture that told her he was just as frustrated about that as she was. He went closer, peering down at David for a moment before he examined the bandage on her arm.

"Are you in pain?" He tipped his head to the script.

"No." That was possibly true, but right now, a good deal of her body was just numb. Probably a result of the adrenaline crash that was already nipping away at her. "What did you find out about the shooter?" she pressed.

The sigh he made was weary as well. "Nothing yet. One of my neighbors caught a glimpse of him. A man wearing dark clothes. That's it. No other description. Still, he might have left his prints or some kind of trace in the garage."

Since this appeared to have been a planned attack, that was a long shot, but Hallie was going to hang on to that possibility. Especially since she didn't have anything else to hang on to.

"The cops checked to see if any of your neighbors had security cams?" Hallie continued.

"Yes. But no one did. That's what I get for living in a low crime neighborhood," he added in a mumble. He dragged in a long breath. "But I do have some good news. Miriam is talking with her lieutenant now, and she's trying to get approval to have your interview delayed until tomorrow. It's after midnight, and you need to get some sleep."

Yes, she could definitely use some rest. Whether she'd be able to get it was anyone's guess. There were times when David still woke up during the night. Plus she'd have to deal with the nightmares and the flashbacks.

Mercy.

She could still hear the sound of those gunshots that'd come way too close to her little boy, and there was no way those sounds would simply go away just because she was exhausted.

"Both our houses are crime scenes," Nick went on, "but I called my brother, and the three of us can stay with him."

His brother was Cullen Brodie, and he was the owner of the Triple R, one of the largest ranches in the county. It was also in Dark River, only a couple of miles from her own house. But Hallie suspected the real reason Nick wanted David and her there was because it was also where Sheriff Leigh Mercer lived. There was plenty of talk around Dark River about Leigh having moved in with Cullen, her fiancé, and Leigh would be able to give Nick backup if he needed it.

"Cullen's okay with us being there?" Hallie asked.

Nick nodded. "There's plenty of room. And, yes, he knows about the danger. A shooter won't be able to just walk up to the place and break in."

No, but with a ranch that size, someone might be able to slip onto the property and blend in with the other ranch hands who worked there. Then, he could just wait for the right moment to attack. It'd be the same, however, if they went back to her place or Nick's. Or even a hotel. That was a reminder of something else she needed to do once she had computer access. She had to find a safe place for David and her.

"Anything on Veronica yet?" she asked.

"I called the hospital while you were getting stitched up. She's still unconscious. They wouldn't give me any other info without a warrant, and I'm not sure I can get one since this isn't my jurisdiction."

True, and Lubbock PD might not approve of an ATF agent stepping into their territory. They would want to be the ones to question Veronica and have any info about her from the medical staff.

"I'm sorry," Nick said, causing her to look up at him.

Hallie groaned when she saw the look in his eyes. Guilt. He was blaming himself for the attack.

"You're not responsible for the shooting," she assured him.

Judging from the profanity he muttered and the way he groaned, he wasn't buying that. "I left you alone to go get your car. What if the gunman had come after you then?"

Hallie opened her mouth to try to give him another assurance, but she stopped. Why hadn't the shooter attacked her then? It would have been perfect timing with Nick gone. Maybe the gunman hadn't arrived yet.

Maybe.

But there was another possibility.

"You think you could have been a target, too?" she asked.

"I'm considering it." He answered so fast that it let her know he'd obviously already given this some thought. "It's possible the shooter decided to take me out because he couldn't be sure what you'd already told me. Of course, that theory means the shooter believed there was something to tell. Something that he wouldn't want others to know."

Yes, and that was yet another unanswered question, but it might indeed all lead back to the militia raid. Perhaps someone tying up loose ends? However, that didn't explain why the shooter had allowed those ends to stay loose for all these months.

The door opened, causing Hallie's heart to jolt again, and she didn't exactly settle much when Miriam walked in. The detective was sporting a stern expression. An exhausted one, too.

"Your interview will be tomorrow at noon," Miriam told Hallie.

Now, Hallie relaxed. Only a little though. Because the interview would be hanging over her head until then. Still, it was better than trying to answer cop questions when she was exhausted and in pain.

"You're still planning on going to Dark River?" the detective asked, shifting her attention to Nick. He nodded. "Okay, I've arranged for two uniforms in a cruiser to follow you there." She checked her watch. "They should be ready to leave in about fifteen minutes."

"Thanks," Nick said, already lifting David's car seat from the floor and setting it on the table next to the baby.

"Don't thank me yet." Miriam lifted a small plastic bag that Hallie instantly recognized as a DNA kit. "I have to do a cheek swab on the baby. My lieutenant insisted. Heck, I have to insist, too."

Hallie felt as if she'd just been punched. She hadn't seen this coming. And she didn't like where it could lead. "The ATF did a DNA test on him already," Hallie snapped. "There was no match on file."

"We need to repeat the test," Miriam insisted, leveling her gaze on Hallie. "We need to try another search."

Yes, this could definitely lead where Hallie didn't want things to. It could point directly to one of David's birth parents. To someone who might have a legal claim on a child she already considered hers. After all, the original DNA test had been done months ago, and it was possible one of David's biological parents had been added to the database since then.

"It's best to know," Miriam told her.

Hallie wasn't sure of that at all, but she knew Miriam could get a court order to obtain the sample. It would delay the results. It wouldn't stop them though. And that's why Hallie stepped aside so that Miriam could glove up and do the cheek swab.

Nick brushed his hand over Hallie's. No doubt trying to comfort her. But there was no comfort in something that could ultimately take this child from her.

Hallie kept her eyes on the baby through the procedure. But David hardly stirred as Miriam did the test and then bagged the two swabs she'd taken.

"Has Steve Fain stayed in touch with you?" Nick asked, directing his question to Miriam.

"He called me just today." Miriam paused. "Why?"

Nick lifted his shoulder. "I'm wondering why he's suddenly so interested in Hallie."

Hallie had to pick back through her memory to connect Steve to Miriam, and she recalled Steve talking about getting together with Miriam and Nick when they'd still been dating.

Miriam studied Nick for a very long moment. "You think Steve had something to do with what happened tonight?"

"I think I want to talk to him about it," Nick countered. "That's why I was wondering if Steve had stayed in touch with you. Not just today but over the past months since he turned in his badge."

Miriam's eyebrow lifted a fraction. "He calls every now and then when he's working on a case that intersects with something I'm investigating." She stopped, huffed. "I've been out with him a couple of times for drinks. Nothing serious," she quickly added. "And I haven't told him anything about an investigation that I wouldn't have told any other PI. Which means I haven't told him much of anything at all."

Nick studied Miriam, too, while Hallie transferred David to his car seat. "What about Ty Levine?" Nick pressed Miriam. "Has he been in touch with you, too?"

"Yes." That was all Miriam said for a couple of seconds. Hallie didn't think she was wrong that the detective was debating how much info to give Nick. And how much to hold back. "He wanted an update on the investigation into Kelsey's death."

"You would have looked into him by now," Nick pointed out. "So what'd you find out?"

Miriam had a couple more seconds of debate before she answered. "I can't confirm that he was ever part of the Brothers of Freedom militia, but I can tell you that Kelsey's cousin was."

That felt like another punch. Because it was an association that could mean Kelsey was indeed David's biological mother. *Could.* It could also just be a bad coincidence.

"What's the cousin's name?" Nick asked.

"Lamar Travers." Since Miriam had known that off the top of her head, it likely meant the detective had already investigated the man.

"Have you talked to him?" Hallie asked.

"Not yet. But I've left him several messages to call me. If he doesn't, I'll start tracking him down."

Hallie very much wanted to track down the man as well. But she hoped this wasn't opening Pandora's box. Because it was entirely possible that this cousin was going to admit that he'd taken David or else Kelsey had handed over the baby to the militia. If she had been paid for giving up her child, then there might be a money trail Hallie could follow.

Miriam checked her watch again. "The officers should have the cruiser in front of the building by now," she said, but before she could move to the door, her phone rang. "It's the hospital," Miriam muttered after she looked at the screen.

Veronica.

The call had to be about her.

Hallie had already lifted David's car seat off the table, but she stopped. Listened. Or rather she tried to listen. Miriam certainly didn't put the call on speaker, and Hallie could only hear the murmuring of the voice on the other end of the line.

"What?" Miriam asked the caller. Her tone was sharp, and she cast an uneasy glance at Hallie. "You believe her?" she added. Paused. "I'll get back to you."

Miriam ended the call but stared at her phone for a

while. When she finally lifted her eyes, Hallie knew this was not going to be good news.

"Did Veronica die?" Hallie asked, but she was afraid to hear the answer.

"No," Miriam said without hesitation. "She's very much alive. And conscious."

The relief loosened some of the muscles in her chest. "I want to see her—"

"No," Miriam snapped. "You won't be seeing her until I get some things cleared up." She stared at Hallie. "Veronica claims that you're the one who tried to kill her."

Chapter Six

Nick gulped down some coffee and wished that he'd gotten a little more sleep. Four hours just hadn't been enough, but he was betting it was still more shut-eye than Hallie had managed. She looked as exhausted as he was.

And worried.

That worried part was coming through loud and clear even though she was smiling and babbling with David as she fed him oatmeal. The baby sat in his infant seat for the meal since there hadn't been a high chair at the Triple R. Something that Cullen had said he'd remedy and that one would be delivered later that morning.

Thankfully, David wasn't clued in to the stress or even the inconvenience of not having his usual things around. That was probably normal for a baby, but Nick figured things weren't going to get easier for Hallie until she figured out what was going on with Veronica. And everything else in her life.

It had taken some fast talking from Nick to stop Miriam from detaining Hallie after the detective had gotten that incriminating call about Veronica. Fast talking and a reminder that Veronica had a head injury and that she had to be mistaken about who had hurt her.

There was also the logistics of such an assault. A point that Nick had drilled home with Miriam. David had been with Hallie at the time of Veronica's attack, and Nick had convinced Miriam that there was no way Hallie would have assaulted a woman and then dumped her with a baby in tow. Plus there was no motive for such an attack. Hallie was adopting David, and there was absolutely no proof that Veronica had objected to that.

When Hallie finished feeding David, she carried the bowl to the sink and then just stood there, staring down at the water as she rinsed the bowl. "I want to try to see Veronica before I have to go back in for the interview with Miriam at one o'clock," she muttered.

It wasn't the first time Hallie had brought up that particular subject. She'd insisted on doing it during the drive to the Triple R in the early hours of the morning. Nick couldn't blame her for wanting the visit with Veronica. The woman had accused her of assault, maybe even attempted murder, and coming on the heels of Kelsey's suspicious death and the attacks, Hallie had to feel as if plenty of bad stuff was piling up on her. And it was. Piling up on him, too, because keeping Hallie and David safe was a huge priority.

"I'd planned on talking to Miriam again this morning," Nick explained, going closer to her. "I might be able to convince her to let me see Veronica. Then, I can question her."

Something that Nick knew Miriam wasn't going to allow Hallie to do. Not when Hallie was a suspect in the assault. As long as Veronica was claiming Hallie had had any part in what'd happened to her, there'd be no visit. Which was a shame. Because Hallie was no doubt already feeling plenty guilty over what'd happened to Veronica, and the guilt and worry would only skyrocket until she was finally allowed to talk to the woman face-to-face.

Hallie turned around, volleying glances between David and him. Her bottom lip trembled a little, but he could also see that she was trying to steady herself. Hard to do though when her life was falling apart.

Well, some aspects of her life were.

When her attention landed on David, the love was there. All over her face. And while that love couldn't erase the other things that were happening, Nick had no doubts that Hallie would be a heck of a lot worse off without the baby.

"Why would Veronica say I'd hurt her?" Hallie asked, and yeah, that bottom lip started to quiver some more.

Nick had given that some thought. In fact, a lot of thought, and it'd been one of the reasons he hadn't gotten much sleep. That and his frustration over the attraction he was feeling for Hallie. An attraction that was plenty strong even though he was dealing with the bone-weary fatigue, the threat of another attack and the investigation to stop anything else from going wrong.

"It's possible the head injury is making Veronica misremember," he said, speculating. "And her attacker could have also drugged her. That could be playing havoc with memories especially if he planted some lies that would point the finger at you."

Hallie's eyes cleared. Her mouth went firm. And she nodded. "You can get her tox screen?"

"I'll try." But he'd do more than that. He'd push to get the results. Because if Veronica had indeed been drugged with something that could have altered her perception or memories, then that would work to clear Hallie's name.

They definitely needed something in her favor.

Nick hadn't spelled out that Miriam might arrest her, but it was a strong possibility. Well, unless he could come up with something in the next five hours that would prevent the cop from doing just that. If Veronica couldn't amend her statement, then Nick would have to use whatever evidence he could find to prove Hallie's innocence.

He looked down at her. Their gazes connected. And he tried to give her some kind of reassurance. It didn't, however, go as he'd planned. Instead of a soothing look, he leaned in and brushed his mouth over hers. Just a touch.

One that packed a wallop.

Nick didn't know who was more surprised by the

reaction—Hallie or him. But there was definite surprise in her eyes. And arousal. Yeah, she was obviously dealing with this unwanted heat, too, and Nick might have given that heat a push with another kiss if he hadn't heard the footsteps. He turned just as Leigh and Cullen came into the kitchen.

Cullen obviously noticed the close contact between them because he lifted an eyebrow. Probably to remind Nick that it wasn't a good time to be thinking about putting his hands on Hallie. The timing did indeed suck, but Nick had no idea how to rid himself of the urgent need that he had for her.

"Thank you again for letting us stay here," Hallie said, her voice breathy and her words rushing together.

"Anytime," Cullen assured her. He went to the baby who was still in his car seat on the floor, and he stooped down and touched his finger to David's belly. The boy gave him a big gummy grin. "The baby supplies should be here any minute now. There's a crib coming, too." He looked up at Hallie. "There'll also be some clothes and toiletries for you since I suspect it'll be a while before you can get back to your house."

Hallie muttered another thank-you, and Nick knew it was heartfelt. He also knew she wasn't exactly comfortable being here and that all the baby supplies and clothes wouldn't change that.

Leigh went to David, too, smiling down at him for a moment before she looked at Hallie. "Your statement about the break-in should be ready for your signature in about an hour."

That was fast since Leigh had only finished the interview right before David had started his breakfast. It'd been a low-key interview, done in the guest room where Hallie and David had spent the night. That'd been a far better location than going into the Dark River Police Department. Still, it had been hard on Hallie to relive the terror of having someone go after David like that.

"Cullen and I were talking," Leigh went on, "about your appointment with Lubbock PD. I considered asking the detective in charge if she'd come out here to talk to you, but I'm figuring she'll want you on her turf."

Miriam would indeed want that. Not only because it'd be following procedure, but she'd want Hallie on the premises in case she had to make an arrest.

"I've already asked Miriam about doing that, and she said no," Nick explained. "Apparently, there aren't enough strings to pull to get Miriam to change her mind. Or rather her lieutenant's mind. He insisted on Hallie showing for the noon interview."

Leigh nodded as if that'd been exactly what she had expected. "Then, Cullen and I think you should consider leaving the baby here with us while you're in Lubbock." Hallie opened her mouth, no doubt to object, but Leigh continued talking. "It's a risk for any of you to be on the road, and David would be safer here. Rosa said she'd be happy to watch him."

Rosa Tyree was Cullen's longtime housekeeper, and

she'd also helped Hallie and David get settled into the guest room. Nick had known the woman for years, and she was as steady as they came.

"It's hard for me to be away from him," Hallie murmured, going to the baby and scooping him up in her arms. She brushed a kiss on the top of his head, causing David to cuddle his face into the crook of her neck. "Especially after everything that's happened."

"Understandable," Cullen agreed. "But I promise you that he'll be safe and well cared for here."

Both of those things were huge. Especially the safe part. Because Leigh was right. It was risky to take David on the drive where the shooter might try to have another go at them. Their attacker had already proven that he didn't mind endangering a child, and he could fire shots into any vehicle they'd be using. A cruiser would be bullet resistant, but shots could still get through.

"There's something else to consider," Leigh continued a moment later. "If the detective takes you into custody today, you'll have to be processed and booked. I know that might be a long shot, but it's still a possibility."

Leigh was hedging some. Because it wasn't a long shot at all. If Miriam's lieutenant pushed for Hallie's arrest, Nick doubted he'd be able to talk the man out of doing just that.

"And if it happens, Lubbock PD will have to call CPS," Leigh went on. "They could take David and put him in a foster home while you're trying to get everything sorted out."

"Nick said he would take him," Hallie blurted out, holding David even closer to her.

"He'd try, I'm sure, but he might get overruled. Even if David needs protective custody, Lubbock PD might not agree on who David should be with," Leigh added. She kept her voice level and calm. The voice of reason. "Miriam and her boss might insist that they can protect him as well as ATF."

"And Nick doesn't have a legal claim to take David," Cullen pointed out to bolster Leigh's argument.

Nick thought about the papers that were at Hallie's house. The ones they hadn't picked up after they'd had to deal with the aftermath of the shooting. He doubted Veronica's signed agreement would be enough to keep David safe from being taken from Hallie.

And that was something Hallie needed to hear.

Nick went to her, taking hold of her shoulders, but David obviously thought this was a fun game because he twisted around and practically leaped into Nick's arms. Despite their situation, Nick smiled, and he took hold of the boy while he added his two cents to convincing her to leave David at the Triple R.

"Even if Miriam doesn't detain you," Nick explained, "CPS might step in anyway. It might not matter that the adoption will be finalized soon. CPS could feel obligated to take temporary custody of him."

He saw that hit home with Hallie. She went stiff, and her breath came out in one shaky gust.

"What if CPS comes here to get him?" Hallie asked. The fear was in her voice and all over her face. "What if they do that while we're in Lubbock?"

"I'll do a temporary order of protective custody," Leigh explained so quickly that it was obvious she'd already worked through this. "I'll say it's an unnecessary risk to move him from the ranch. That's the truth. I can even assign deputies to stay here to assure CPS that we're taking steps to keep David safe. It wouldn't hurt for me to point out, too, that any foster family who takes him could end up in danger as well."

Cullen made a sound of agreement. "My ranch hands have been alerted to keep watch for any suspicious activity, and the security system will stay on. It's a good system with exterior cameras and motion detectors. I upgraded after I had some trouble here at the ranch a couple of months ago."

The trouble had been a murder, and the investigation had thrown Cullen and Leigh together. Nick knew that Leigh and his brother could handle the worst kind of danger. That was another plus in having David stay put.

Hallie stayed quiet a moment. "You've got a solid argument. And plan. Something I should have already come up with," she added. "Because you're right. It isn't a good idea for David to be on the road, in Lubbock or with anyone who doesn't know how to protect him."

Nick felt the muscles ease up in his shoulders and

chest. It wouldn't be easy for Hallie to leave the baby behind here at the Triple R, but it was better than the alternative. Nick figured he was just as haunted as Hallie was by the attack that could have hurt David.

"Do you think we can do anything to speed up the trip to Lubbock?" Hallie asked, turning to Nick. "I want to spend as little time away from David as possible."

Nick nodded. He was on the same page as she was about this. Also, it was best for them to be with the boy since Hallie and he could provide another layer of protection to the measures Leigh and Cullen were already taking.

"I'll call Miriam and explain to her what's going on," Nick answered. He couldn't imagine Miriam pressing for Hallie to bring the baby, but even if she did, it wasn't going to happen. "I'll also see if I can get any updates on Veronica."

Specifically, Nick wanted the woman's tox results. He also wanted to talk to her, and he needed to work out a way for that to happen. It was possible he could convince Miriam that Veronica was a key witness in finding the person who'd tried to kill Hallie and him. Which she probably was. After all, the person who'd attacked Veronica had likely also been the one who'd shot at Hallie and him.

"You can use the office just up the hall," Cullen instructed when Nick took out his phone to start making the calls.

Nick turned to take his brother up on the offer, but

his phone rang before he could even take a step. He frowned because he didn't recognize the number on the screen.

"Agent Nick Brodie?" the man said the moment he answered.

"Yes. Who is this?"

"I need to talk to Hallie," the caller insisted. "She's not answering her phone, and it's important I get in touch with her."

"Who is this?" Nick repeated, and this time he made sure it sounded like an order, not just a request.

The caller certainly didn't jump right in with an answer. And that gave Nick a bad feeling. Of course, with everything that was going on, he hadn't had a lot of good feelings.

"This is Darius Lawler," the caller finally said.

Nick didn't have to dig through his memory to recall that name. And it wasn't an especially good recollection, either. Darius was the criminal informant who'd given the ATF insider info for the militia raid. He'd then disappeared right after the raid had gone south with Nick and Hallie getting shot.

"Darius Lawler," Nick repeated out loud so that Hallie would know who was on the phone. Her eyes widened, and she moved closer so she could hear. "I thought you might be dead," Nick told the man.

"Nearly was. That's why I gotta talk to Hallie. Can you get a message to her and tell her I got something important to tell her?"

"Why don't you let us take the baby while you talk?" Cullen suggested in a whisper, and when he reached out his hands for David, the baby went right to him. "We'll be in the family room," he added, tipping his head in the direction of the massive room just off the kitchen.

"You there, Brodie?" Darius snarled.

"I'm here," Nick assured him, and he put the call on speaker. "Why do you need to talk to Hallie?"

"That's between her and me. Like I said, I got things to tell her."

Nick motioned for her to stay quiet. After all, Darius had a criminal record, and he'd been a member of the militia. The very militia that he'd ratted out when the ATF had offered him money to do just that. Darius had helped with the raid, too, more or less. More in that he'd given the ATF the layout of the militia camp and the leaders' names. What he hadn't mentioned were the babies, and Nick very much wanted to know why the man hadn't done that.

"Hallie's no longer an ATF agent," Nick told Darius.

"I know. That's why I think I can trust her. Not sure I can trust you or anybody else with a badge."

Nick had had several conversations with Darius, and he'd never heard the man mention a distrust of law enforcement. Then again, the guy was a criminal. One Nick definitely didn't trust enough to let him know that Hallie was with him.

"You disappeared right after the raid," Nick reminded him. "Why?"

"I had my reasons," Darius said, and then he huffed.

"Did those reasons have to do with the babies the militia was holding so they could sell them?" Nick demanded.

"No." Darius seemed shocked that Nick would even suggest that. Of course, it might be faked shock to cover up his guilt. "And I'm not getting into this with you. Where's Hallie?"

Nick ignored the man's demand and went with one of his own. Since Darius didn't seem keen to talk about the babies, he might be willing to discuss something else. "Tell me about Ty Levine. Was he in the militia?"

Darius cursed. "No, he wasn't. But I know who he is. I've been keeping my ear to the ground, and I hear things."

That grabbed Nick's attention. "Oh, yeah? Like what?"

This time Darius wasn't so fast with an answer. "I need to get into that with Hallie. I like her. I think I can trust her."

Hallie had indeed dealt with Darius during the prep for the raid, but Nick hadn't noticed the CI showing her any more respect or attention than he had anyone else.

"Why do you think you can trust her?" Nick asked, and he smoothed out his tone some. If he continued to snap and snarl, Darius might just hang up.

"Because I think she figured out that things were messed up in the ATF and she got out. Turned in her badge and just got out before all that mess could come back on her."

Hallie stayed quiet, but she was staring at the phone as if trying to decide what the heck Darius meant by that.

"What mess are you talking about?" Nick asked, and because he thought Darius might just make another demand to speak to Hallie, Nick made the question multiple choice. "The black market baby ring? The fact that Hallie got shot during the raid? The ATF—"

"All of it," Darius blurted out, but then he huffed again. "Look, I don't want to get into this with you."

"Too late," Nick muttered. He stopped and tried to figure out the best way to go about this. Just in case the man truly did have something important to say, he didn't want Darius clamming up. "Is there something about the ATF you want to tell Hallie?"

"Yeah. Not you though. Just her. It has to be her, or I'm not saying anything else."

Nick paused again. Debated. Then, he gave Hallie the nod. "I'm here, Darius. Anything you say to me, you can also say to Nick."

"Hallie? That's really you?" Darius asked.

"It's really me, and yes, I got out of the ATF. Out of the mess," she added, and Nick knew she had carefully chosen her words.

The breath that Darius took seemed to be one of relief. "Then, you know there's trouble brewing," the man said like gospel.

"I do, and I need you to tell me what you know about it. I need your help." Hallie made it sound like a plea.

"Okay," Darius answered after a long pause. "Okay," he repeated as if gathering his thoughts. "I left the compound after the raid because I thought somebody was going to kill me. I thought you might get killed, too, since you were digging so hard to find the truth."

"I'm still digging," Hallie assured him. "Help me do that. Who did you think might try to kill us?"

Darius's next pause was even longer. "You can find proof if you dig into bank records. There'll be payments he took from Greer Boggs."

Greer had been the main leader of the militia. And he'd also died in a gunfight during the raid. Nick was certain of that because he'd seen the body.

"He?" Hallie and Nick pressed at the same time. It was Hallie who continued. "Who took payments from Greer and why?"

"They were for the babies," Darius answered. "He sold them to Greer, and Greer paid him."

Everything inside Nick went still, but he didn't demand more info. He just reined in the flood of emotions and waited for Darius to keep talking. If he started firing off questions, it might spook the man, and he might clam up.

Darius finally did continue. "All the payments were in cash, but there was a lot of it. I figure he put it in his bank account. Or maybe hid it like an investment. Anyway, I believe he's the one who messed up the raid and got you and Nick shot. He's the one who made sure I didn't get any intel on the kids to pass on to you."

"Who?" Hallie demanded. "Who sold the babies to Greer?"

Darius groaned. "Please don't tell him I told you. He'll kill me. I know he will."

"Who?" Hallie repeated. "I need a name so I can start clearing up this *mess*."

"Former ATF agent Steve Fain," Darius muttered, and he ended the call.

Chapter Seven

Hallie figured she owed Steve Fain some thanks for helping to get her mind off the fact that she'd left David at the Triple R Ranch. Ditto for helping her get her mind off the grueling interview she'd just done with Miriam. However, Hallie had no thanks for the man who could be behind the attacks. If Steve was responsible, then he needed to pay and pay hard.

"Still no answer," Nick grumbled when he tried to call Steve again.

Hallie had lost count of how many times Nick had tried to reach the former ATF agent, but the attempts were now in double digits. Nick had left plenty of messages, too, but Steve had yet to respond to any of them. Maybe because he knew he was now a person of interest in multiple felonies, including attempted murder and endangering a child?

Of course, it was possible that Darius had it all wrong.

She didn't want to believe that though. Hallie wanted to latch on to the possibility that they had a real suspect, and that if they could get Steve to confess, it would put an end to the danger. That way, she wouldn't have to leave her baby behind while she went off to be grilled by Lubbock PD. Wouldn't have to deal with the terror that Nick, David, Veronica and she could be attacked again.

Nick left another message for Steve to call him ASAP, and he looked at her, no doubt to make sure she wasn't about to fall apart. He was in the now open door of the interrogation room. A place he'd been since Miriam had finished the interview and then gone to her lieutenant's office to discuss Hallie's fate. Miriam hadn't spelled out the "fate" part, but Hallie knew that's what was happening.

It was entirely possible that the lieutenant, or even Miriam, would press to have her taken into custody.

Hallie tried to push that possibility aside. Tried to push away her worry for David, too. She needed a clear head so she could think and sort through what her next step should be.

"We have to get a look at Steve's financials," she said.

Not for the first time, either. On the drive to Lubbock, both Nick and she had tried to figure out a way to go about doing that. They wouldn't get permission or a warrant solely on the word of a criminal informant. So, they needed a whole lot more, and it felt as if there was a ticking clock on what they should be getting done. If Steve was the shooter, the one responsible for all those black market babies, then the sooner he was arrested, the better.

"Leigh could maybe help us get into his bank records," Nick suggested. "If Darius can give us specific details and dates about payments."

Yes, but for that to happen, Steve would have to return their calls. So far, he hadn't done that. Ditto for Kelsey's cousin, Lamar Travers, who had been a member of the militia. It was beyond frustrating that she couldn't talk to any of those three men while she was stuck here at the Lubbock Police Department. If Miriam and her lieutenant cleared her, Nick and she could at least go to Steve's place. Of course, that'd mean delaying their trip back to the ranch, but it could be time well spent.

"We should talk to Ty again," Hallie suggested. "He might be able to help us get in touch with Lamar."

Yes, it was a long shot that Ty would know the whereabouts of his ex-girlfriend's cousin, but pretty much everything they had right now was a long shot.

Nick made a sound of agreement, and he pulled up something on his phone to show her. It was a photo of a young dark-haired man with plenty of scruff on his jaw. "That's Lamar. I don't remember seeing him the night of the raid."

Hallie studied his face and picked back through the memories of that horrible time. "Neither do I. I also don't recall his name coming up in the investigation that led up to the raid." She looked at Nick. "You think Miriam would be willing to share any info she has on him?"

"I'll ask. I've initiated a thorough search on him

through the ATF. There are still some militia members around who might be willing to spill something. If there's anything to spill," he added.

True. Since Lamar had belonged to the militia, he obviously wasn't squeaky clean, but that didn't mean he'd had anything to do with the babies or the attacks.

"I've also asked for a warrant to bring in Darius for questioning," Nick went on. "Getting the warrant won't be a problem, not with his record, but finding him might be. Darius had managed to stay under the radar all these months."

"Yes," she quietly agreed. "And according to what Darius told us, the only reason he surfaced was because he was afraid Steve was going to kill him." She heard the skepticism in her own tone and groaned. "It's possible that Darius told us that to deflect guilt off himself."

Nick didn't argue with that, and it meant that Darius was now in the running as one of their suspects. Him, Steve, Ty and Kelsey's cousin. Too bad there wasn't a lick of evidence to arrest any of them. But someone was certainly guilty of the attacks. Maybe of murdering Kelsey, too. If the woman was actually murdered, that was. Hallie hadn't seen any proof so far to verify that.

Her phone dinged with a text, and even though it was a soft sound, hearing the jolt of it shot through her like a bullet, proving that her nerves were way too close to the surface. Those nerves went up a significant notch when she saw that the text was from Rosa.

Sweet heaven. Had something happened to David?

Nick must have noticed her alarmed body language because he hurried to her. Her hand was trembling when she pressed the text to read it, and she saw the picture. It was of David sleeping in the crib that'd been delivered to the ranch. They'd set it up in the sitting room attached to the guest room Hallie was using so that David wouldn't be too far from her at night. He looked totally zonked out and at peace.

Sweet baby sleeping, Rosa had messaged. Just wanted you to know that he's doing fine.

Hallie smiled, and she felt some of her anxiety fade. She ran her fingers over the screen, outlining that precious little face. She missed him more than she'd ever thought it possible to miss anyone or anything.

"You'll be able to get back to him soon," Nick remarked. He smiled, too, when he looked at the baby.

She definitely wanted that to be *soon*, but she feared it might not happen when Miriam came back into the interview room. One look at her, and Hallie could see that the detective wasn't sporting a happy expression.

Hallie sent a quick reply to Rosa, thanking the woman for sending the photo and instructing her to tell David that she loved him when he woke up. Then, she put her phone away and braced herself for the worst.

"You're not under arrest," Miriam said right off the bat. "At this time anyway," she quickly added, and in that span of a couple of seconds that'd it'd taken the detective to tack that last bit on, Hallie's hopes had gone from soaring to crashing.

Nick, however, went with the anger. A thick layer of it. "After everything that's happened, you can't believe Hallie had anything to do with Veronica's injury or Kelsey's death," he snarled.

Miriam met his hard gaze. "As a matter of fact, I don't believe she's guilty. Neither does my lieutenant. But the fact remains that Veronica has accused Hallie of assaulting her."

"Veronica has a head injury," Nick pointed out before Hallie could speak. And yes, he was still snarling.

"I'm well aware of that," Miriam countered. "I'm also aware that Veronica had been drugged when she was attacked." She handed Nick the paper she'd been holding. "Those are her tox results. They just came in."

Hallie looked at the report. And cursed under her breath. Because someone had given Veronica a date rape drug. Lots of it, too. Plenty enough to have altered her memory. Or even erased it.

"Was she raped?" Hallie came out and asked while she prayed that it wasn't true.

"No," Miriam stated. "There were no signs of sexual assault. But I'm guessing her attacker knew that Rohypnol would make it a whole lot harder to recall much of anything about who actually did this to her."

"You're thinking the person who drugged her planted the notion that I attacked her," Hallie concluded, and when Miriam verified that with a crisp nod, Hallie wanted to curse again. Someone had wanted to make sure she got blamed for what'd happened to Veronica.

Probably the same someone who'd tried to kill her at Nick's house.

"Veronica knows she was drugged?" Nick asked. He'd throttled back on his anger and was studying the tox results.

"Yes. The doctor told her about fifteen minutes ago," Miriam replied. "She's upset about it but doesn't recall being dosed. Not that surprising since she remembers very little about the attack."

"Does Veronica know that Hallie wasn't the one who hurt her?" Nick pressed.

"She's apparently starting to come around to that. She admits that it's not something Hallie would do." The detective shifted her attention to Hallie. "Veronica says she wants to see you."

Hallie reached for her purse. "Let's go," she insisted.

But Miriam stopped Hallie by stepping in front of her. "There are some conditions for the visit. The doctor doesn't want Veronica getting upset so if that happens, you'll be ordered to leave. Apparently, Veronica's blood pressure is way too high, and the doctor is concerned."

Hallie was concerned, too, but considering everything Veronica had been through, it was understandable that she'd have some health problems. Understandable as well that the doctor would want to keep her as calm as possible.

"There's another rule," Miriam continued when Hallie tried to go around her. "Don't press Veronica too hard about what happened to her. According to the doctor, that could implant images and even false memories in her head. He'd rather her recall the incident at her own pace. Then, what she does remember is more likely to be what actually happened."

Hallie went still. It was possible that Veronica had seen her attacker. And that she could identify him. So, no, Nick and she wouldn't press the woman, but Hallie hoped that Veronica's mind would clear soon because any little detail she could give them might help.

"I can have a couple of uniform cops follow you to the hospital," Miriam offered, "but I'd rather not tie them up by having them go back to Dark River with you."

"Sheriff Mercer is sending deputies to escort us back to my brother's ranch," Nick said, adding a thank-you to Miriam for the temporary police protection.

Hallie thanked her as well. Having cops nearby would maybe deter the shooter from trying to kill them. But it was also a reminder that Veronica could still be in danger.

"Do you still have a guard on Veronica?" Hallie asked.

Miriam nodded. "She's in room 212, and she'll be covered as long as she's there. Since she lives here in Lubbock, I'll also offer her protection after she's released from the hospital." The detective paused. "Follow the rules on not pushing Veronica, but if you can work it in, try to find out who attacked her. And why he left her alive."

Hallie had already given some thought to the last one. Nick had, too. Considering that Veronica had been assaulted and dumped near her home, it would have been easy for her attacker to simply kill her instead of kidnapping her.

"I'm guessing he left her alive to either set up Hallie," Nick said, "or because he got whatever information he wanted."

Miriam's eyebrow came up again. "And what info would that be?"

"Something related to David. Maybe his adoption or it could have something to do with why he was in that black market baby ring."

Yes, Hallie had been trying to wrap her mind around that, but it was like looking at a puzzle with key pieces missing. Pieces that any one of their suspects—Steve, Ty, Darius or Lamar—might be able to fill in. But Veronica could possibly help as well.

"Can we go to the hospital now?" Hallie asked.

Miriam didn't question why the sudden hurry. She certainly knew just how important this visit with Veronica could be.

Nick and she followed Miriam as she led them through the bullpen and to the front where Nick was parked. There was already a cruiser with two cops waiting behind his SUV. They both thanked Miriam again and hurried out to the vehicle.

Apparently, Nick knew the way to the hospital because he didn't put an address in the GPS. He just started driving. And keeping watch. His lawman's gaze fired all around them, looking for any signs of the shooter. Riding shotgun, Hallie did the same, but the problem was there were too many people out and about. Lots of faces to pick through.

And try to decide if one of them was a would-be killer.

Hallie didn't want to be attacked again, but part of her wished if there was going to be another attempt on her life that it would happen when David was safe at the ranch. Then again, she didn't want to put Nick at risk, either. Too bad she couldn't figure a way to keep him safe, too.

It took them less than ten minutes to get to the hospital, and Nick parked as close to the ER doors as he could manage. The two cops got out of their cruiser, walking with them to the door, but they left as soon as Nick and she were inside. They didn't waste any time heading to the second floor.

The hospital wasn't that big, and the moment they got off the elevator, Hallie spotted the police guard outside room 212. "I just got a call saying you were coming," the beefy cop said. "I'll need to see some ID though before I can let you in."

Hallie was glad that he'd insisted on taking that security measure, and she took out her driver's license. Nick used his badge and credentials. The cop studied them, something else that pleased Hallie. He didn't give the IDs a mere cursory glance before he finally stepped to the side and opened the door.

Veronica was in the bed, an IV in one arm and an automatic blood pressure cuff on the other. She was pale, no color at all in her face except for the nasty bruise on her cheekbone. It didn't look as if it'd come from a punch but maybe from a fall. The bandage around her head was no doubt to protect the injury that had rendered her unconscious.

"Hallie," she said, her voice as weak as she looked. "Is David all right? The detective told me he was, but I didn't know if she was saying that so I wouldn't get upset."

"David's fine," Hallie assured her. "He's safe."

Veronica's breath swooshed out in obvious relief, and she closed her eyes for a moment. "Thank God." When she opened her eyes, she fixed her gaze to Hallie. "I'm so sorry I told the cops that you'd been the one to hurt me."

Hallie waved that off. Yes, it'd stung, but it was more important now to focus on moving forward and learning the truth.

"You were confused." Hallie went closer, sliding her hand over Veronica's to give it a gentle squeeze. "Veronica, this is ATF agent Nick Brodie."

Some recognition went through Veronica's pale gray eyes. Not a good kind of recognition, either. Veronica started to scramble back, but Hallie stopped her by gently taking hold of her shoulder.

"The call you got about Nick was wrong," Hallie told her. "He's not dirty, and he didn't have anything to do with your attack."

"You're sure?" Veronica asked, her voice quavering.

"Positive." Hallie shifted so she could look Veronica straight in the eyes. "Nick's helping me, and he's working hard to keep David safe."

Veronica muttered those last three words, repeating them several times as if trying to make it sink in. "You're really helping Hallie protect David?" Veronica asked him.

"I am," Nick said. "I'm trying to keep Hallie safe, too." He stayed back, by the door, maybe because he didn't want to spook Veronica more than she already was. "You can help with that if you tell us what happened to you."

Veronica shook her head, touching her fingers to her temple. "The memories are all mixed up. It's like I'm looking at things through dirty glasses. Everything's smeared and out of focus."

"We might still be able to get some details through the smears," Hallie assured her. "Just go over what you do remember."

After a long pause, Veronica nodded. "I got that call warning me about Nick, but the caller wouldn't say who he was."

"He?" Nick pressed.

"Maybe a he," the woman amended after she gave it some thought. "I can't be positive, but I think it might have been a man. The person told me that Nick was part of the black market baby ring at the militia. Then, I called you." She stopped, her gaze drilling into Hallie. "That really happened, right? I called you?"

"You did, and you asked me to come over," Hallie told her. "When I got there, you were gone."

Veronica took a moment, obviously trying to process that. "So, the person must have kidnapped me shortly after I spoke to you."

Hallie made a sound of agreement. "It took me about a half hour to drive to your house. The front door was open so I looked in. I called out for you, but you weren't there. You were missing for several hours, and then someone found you on the side of the road."

Hallie left it at that because she didn't want to push Veronica. She wanted to give her some time to process what Hallie was telling her. And maybe remember critical details about her abduction.

Veronica stared at her as if that would help with the memories. "I don't know what happened to me. Not after I called you. Not until I woke up here in the hospital. I know you wouldn't have done this to me." She touched the bandage on her head. "But I keep hearing this voice that said you did."

So, it was true. Her abductor had tried to plant false memories.

"Can you recall if the voice was male or female?" Nick asked. What he didn't do was point out to Veronica that what she'd heard was the voice of her attacker.

Veronica's forehead bunched up for a couple of seconds. "I can't be sure. It's like a whisper. Barely audible."

Hallie figured that'd been done on purpose. No sense giving Veronica anything she could use to ID him or her. But maybe the kidnapper had done something that Veronica would remember later.

"Did you pick up on some other sounds?" Hallie asked. "Background noise, maybe? Or maybe this person talking to someone else?"

Veronica pressed her fingers to the side of her head as if trying to push out the info. "No, I'm sorry. Nothing like that."

"Did the person ever lift you or pick you up?" Nick asked, and Hallie knew he was trying to home in on the kidnapper's size.

"No," Veronica repeated, and this time her eyes watered. "I should remember that. I should remember all of it. This person could have killed me, and I don't even know who to look for."

The blood pressure cuff began its automatic reading again, and when Hallie saw the numbers come on the screen, she knew it was time for Nick and her to go. Veronica's blood pressure was creeping up, and this conversation was only adding to her stress. It was best to give the woman a little more time to try to remember what'd happened to her.

"Everything will be okay," Hallie tried to reassure her. "Nick and I are going to find who did this to you.

In the meantime, you're safe. The police guard will be right outside your door."

Veronica nodded, the gesture weary and layered with fatigue. She muttered another "I'm sorry" as Hallie and Nick stepped out. The guard was still there. But he wasn't alone.

Steve Fain was standing across from the cop. Judging from the crossed arms and the way he was leaning against the wall, Steve was waiting for him.

Waiting and riled.

"I got your messages," Steve snarled. "You want to talk about that here or somewhere else?"

Nick returned Steve's snarl with a glare, and he positioned himself between Steve and her. He motioned for Steve to follow them to the end of the hall. It wasn't exactly private, not with medical staff going in and out of the rooms and with the cop only about fifteen feet away. Still, Hallie would take lack of privacy over going outside where Nick and she would be easy targets. Maybe an easy target from Steve himself.

"Darius." Nick threw that out there before Steve had a chance to say anything.

Steve's shoulders went back. "What about him? Is he the reason you insisted on speaking to me?"

"He is," Nick agreed. "And he claims you were a dirty ATF agent and the person responsible for the black market baby ring going on in the militia."

Steve stared at him a long time, saying nothing, but Hallie saw the anger flare through the man's eyes. "Darius is a liar. A criminal. Or did you forget that, huh? He'd say whatever it takes to get himself out of hot water or for payment of some ready cash."

"There's no cash involved in this, and he's not in hot water. Well, not with the law anyway, but he believes you're trying to kill him to cover up your involvement in the baby ring." Nick paused and leveled his glare at Steve. "Were you involved, Steve?"

Groaning and cursing, Steve jammed his fist against the wall. Not exactly a punch but close, and Hallie figured the man would have preferred hitting Nick or Darius rather than the wall.

"No," Steve snapped, and he had to get his teeth unclenched before he could continue. "I was a clean ATF agent just like you." He volleyed a quick glare at Hallie before fixing his attention on Nick. "I didn't know about those babies before our raid, and I'm sure as hell not trying to kill a criminal informant. Even one who's telling lies about me."

"Then, why would Darius say those things?" Nick demanded. "Because I'm not buying that he grabbed those accusations out of thin air. Like I said, there's no money angle. Nothing to gain for him that I can see."

"Maybe there is something to gain," Steve grumbled. He paused. "Did Darius happen to say if he'd been in touch with Ty Levine?"

Hallie continued to keep watch around them, but she moved slightly closer to Steve. "Darius knows Ty?"

"Yeah," he snapped. "Probably," Steve amended on

another huff. "It's all connected, you see. I can't prove it, but it's connected. I'm sure of it."

"Explain that," Nick demanded.

Steve's glare eased away, and in its place, Hallie saw the expression of a man who was dreading what he was about to tell them. "I can't prove it," Steve repeated, "but I believe Darius and Ty knew each other through the militia. I think Darius is covering for Ty because they're friends. Or, hell, maybe they're making these wild claims just because they want to put the screws to me."

"And why would they do that?" Hallie asked, certain that Nick had been about to press for the same thing.

The dread in Steve's face increased, and he glanced away. "Because Ty's worried I might be able to put his sorry butt in jail, that's why. Right before Kelsey's death, she told me she wanted to come clean about Ty and her. I pushed her to tell me what that meant, but she clammed up and said it wasn't the right time, that the truth would just stir up a lot of trouble for Ty."

Hallie mentally went through all of that and figured out where she thought this was going. "Are you saying you believe Ty and Kelsey sold or gave their baby to the militia?"

Steve finally looked up, meeting her eyes. "That's exactly what I'm saying. I believe the two of them sold the child, and I think that's why Kelsey's dead."

"And you believe Ty killed her?" Nick asked. "To silence her about the baby?"

Steve lifted his shoulder. "Either Ty or Darius could have done it. I believe Ty and Kelsey gave their baby to Darius to bring to the militia. That means Darius could be arrested for his part in the black market baby ring. Ty, too. So, I think they'd teamed up to try to cover for each other."

It was an interesting theory. Maybe more than a theory. Hallie could see things playing out that way. Being involved in the baby ring wouldn't have put either Darius or Ty in jail for life, but if there was any proof they tipped the militia about the raid, that could result in some extra charges. Serious ones. Considering that people had died and two agents had been shot, Ty and Darius could end up behind bars for a long time.

But there was something off here.

Something that Steve wasn't saying.

Nick obviously picked up on it because he spoke before Hallie could say anything. "Why would Kelsey tell you that she wanted to come clean about Ty and her?" Nick demanded.

Yes, something was definitely off. Steve looked away again, obviously dodging their gazes, and he muttered some profanity under his breath. "Don't read anything into it," Steve growled. "I didn't kill her."

"But?" Nick snarled.

That brought back Steve's glare, and this time it was laced with a mixture of defiance and shame. "I was having an affair with Kelsey."

That caused a bad feeling to wash over Hallie. "For

how long?" she asked. Not a demand though. Her voice was barely above a whisper.

Steve certainly didn't jump to answer that, and he scrubbed his hand over his face. "Long enough. It wasn't exclusive," he quickly added. "She was also seeing Ty at the same time. And maybe others." He looked at Hallie again and then cursed. "Kelsey told me it's possible that I'm David's father."

Chapter Eight

Kelsey told me it's possible that I'm David's father.

That confession had been going through Nick's mind for hours. On the drive back to the ranch and afterward when he'd been working on the investigation. Even though Hallie had spent some of that time with David, it was no doubt weighing heavily on her mind, too.

Steve had walked out of the hospital shortly after delivering that bombshell, and he hadn't bothered to offer an apology as to why he hadn't fessed up sooner to the affair. Maybe because he was embarrassed at having had sex with the much younger woman, but it probably had more to do with the fact that this now made him a suspect in Kelsey's suspicious death. Cops always had to look at the lover or spouse when someone was killed.

And that's exactly what Miriam was doing right now.

There was no way Nick would have kept Steve's confession under wraps, so he'd called Miriam once Hallie and he had gotten back to the Triple R. After hearing the recap of the conversation they'd had with Steve, Miriam was not only eager to bring Steve in for an interview, she would use the man's confession to get a warrant for his financials. If Darius was right, then there might be evidence of Steve's involvement in the baby market operation. Payment for the sale of the babies.

Nick seriously doubted that Miriam would get all the answers she needed from an interview with Steve, and that's why he was doing some digging of his own. Along with leaving yet more messages for Darius, Lamar and Ty to call him. Maybe learning about Kelsey's affair with Steve had set Ty off and caused him to murder her. Even though both Ty and Steve had said they hadn't been exclusive with Kelsey, that didn't mean jealousy hadn't played into this.

As well as DNA.

And that was another problem.

Nick read through the DNA results that the ATF had gathered from the babies they'd recovered during the raid. There'd been no match for David, and if Steve was his biological father, then there should have been. All ATF agents were required to have their DNA on file. That meant maybe Steve wasn't the baby's father after all. Although it was also possible that someone had tampered with the results.

If so, that pointed right back to Steve as well.

Yeah, Nick really wanted a look at the man's financials.

He glanced up from his laptop when he heard the footsteps, and several moments later, Hallie came into the room. She looked tired. And worried. Nick was right there with her. Too little sleep and too much stress could muddle the mind.

So could this heat between them.

Heat that Nick wanted to push aside, but every time he saw her, it was there. Mercy, he needed to figure out a way to deal with what he was feeling, and he had to ignore suggestions from certain parts of his body. Bad suggestions. Nudges to kiss her. And take her to bed.

"I just got David down for the night," she said, stepping closer to him. She lifted the baby monitor to show him the child sacked out in his crib. "I can work unless he wakes up."

Nick checked his watch. It was barely eight o'clock, but that was probably the time that babies often went to bed. Too bad he couldn't coax Hallie into getting some sleep as well, but she looked wired. Ditto for him. It had been a hellish long day, but they still had plenty to do.

Hallie went closer to the desk, peering down at his laptop screen. She didn't groan when she saw the DNA report, but a soft strangled sound came from deep within her throat.

"The results from the DNA that Miriam took from David should be back later tonight or tomorrow," Nick told her. "We'll know more then."

"More," she repeated, and now she did groan. "Steve could have tampered with the DNA results so no one would know he's David's father. He could have done that shortly after the raid or even later."

Yeah, Steve could have. Kelsey wasn't a minor so he

wouldn't have been trying to cover any statutory rape charges, but it was possible that Steve hadn't wanted any questions about why his son was in the hands of the militia. A militia with plans to sell the baby. Now, that very well would have resulted in charges.

"I don't want Steve to have a claim to David," Hallie murmured, and her voice was filled with the hurt she was feeling over that possibility.

Nick felt the hurt, too. David wasn't his, but he definitely felt a connection to the baby. Felt a connection to Hallie as well. Of course, that particular link had been there for a while, and it was gaining strength fast. Not just because of the attraction, though that was playing into it for sure. But also because Hallie was in a very vulnerable place right now, and he needed to keep David and her safe.

When Nick pulled her into his arms, Hallie sighed and melted against him. "I can't lose David."

"You won't." He hoped that was a promise he could keep. "If Steve is a DNA match, we'll deal with it." How exactly, Nick didn't know, but he damn sure wouldn't hand over a child to a person who might be a criminal.

He brushed a kiss on the top of her head, causing her to look up at him. Their gazes connected. Held. He could feel himself getting lost in her eyes, and that wasn't a good idea. Not now, not when they had so much on their plates.

Nick moved back. Or rather that's what he tried to do. But Hallie's arms went around him, and she held on, pulling him back to her. She didn't stop there, either. She slid her hand around the back of his neck, drawing him down to her so she could kiss him.

Oh, man. The heat was like a punch to the gut. It definitely got his attention, and it wasn't a good kind of attention, either. The taste of her slid into the heat, making him want more, more, more.

She gave him more.

Hallie deepened the kiss and tightened the grip of the arm she still had around his waist. Tightened and brought him closer. Until they were pressed against each other. He could feel her breasts against his chest. Could feel her body already pulsing with need.

With what little control he could manage to keep a leash on, he turned her until he had her anchored against the desk. Even with the heat though, he was mindful of her stitches. Mindful, too, that this wasn't going to go past the kissing stage. Even if every part of him wanted the *more* to lead to sex.

Nick did some deepening on the kiss, too. And he touched. Sliding his hand between them to cup her breast. He wanted more than just a touch. He wanted his mouth on her there. Everywhere. And his body had a reaction to that, too. He went as hard as stone.

When he swiped his thumb over her erect nipple, Hallie moaned, and it had a bad effect on him. Because it seemed as if that silky sound of pleasure was an invitation to move this to the next step.

And they couldn't.

He mentally repeated that to himself, and the sound he made darn sure wasn't silky or soft. It was more of a frustrated growl, but he finally forced himself to tear his mouth from hers. He also stepped back so that he couldn't feel the heat of her body against his or be tempted to touch her again.

With her breath gusting, she blinked several times like a woman coming out of a dream. Hallie didn't try to pull him back to her. Thank goodness. There was no way he could have resisted if she had. So, it was a good thing that each of them had at least a little common sense when it came to the ache and need that this attraction had caused.

"You got my mind off the DNA," she muttered.

Nick managed a smile, and this time when he brushed his mouth over hers, he kept it chaste. Well, as chaste as mouth to mouth could possibly be with Hallie. There was still a punch to it. Heck, breathing had a punch to it whenever she was around.

"Now, I need to take your mind off that." Hallie smiled, too, and brushed her fingers over his erection.

Nick nearly lost his breath, and his eyes might have crossed, but it was good to hear Hallie chuckle at his male reaction. With the danger breathing down their necks, it was nice to have this moment with her. A moment that ended though when she stepped away and went back to his laptop.

He expected her to get that troubled look when she read through the DNA report, but Hallie seemed to shift into law enforcement mode. All business. And she frowned as her gaze skirted over the words in the report.

"If Steve didn't tamper with David's DNA," she said, "it's possible someone else in the ATF did. Maybe someone Ty or Darius paid off."

Nick had already considered that. "Lamar could have done the paying off, too, if he was trying to cover up something, and it wouldn't have necessarily been payment to anyone in the ATF."

She nodded, made a sound of agreement. "Whoever did this could have gotten to somebody in the lab." Hallie paused, sighed, and that did carry the troubled tone. "Or it could have just been screwed up. Mistakes happen, and there was a lot going on that night."

True. But this didn't feel like a mistake. It felt like a cover-up. And that pointed Nick right back to Steve. He had been on scene, and he could have tampered with any evidence during or even after the raid. Which, of course, brought them back to square one again. So many suspects and not a lot of info to help them zero in on the right person.

"I texted Miriam about a half hour ago," Nick explained, "and asked her for an update. She's had no luck getting the warrant for Steve's financials. He's fighting it," he added after he paused.

Hallie jumped right on that. "Which means he could have something to hide."

That was possible, but if Steve was truly innocent, then maybe he just objected to the cops poking into his bank account. Especially since the poking meant the cops considered him a suspect in what could turn out to be a long list of felonies.

"Miriam did have an update on Veronica," Nick went on. Hallie's head whipped up, her attention zooming to him. "Veronica's blood pressure is down, and since her physical injuries aren't posing any serious medical concerns, she could be released from the hospital as early as tomorrow afternoon. She still doesn't remember any more about her attack, but her doctor is going to have her talk with a psychiatrist. Sometimes, they can use hypnosis to recover trauma memories."

He could tell that gave Hallie some hope. Of course, it wouldn't be pleasant for Veronica to have to go back through something horrific like that. Even in memories, it would be hard. But the woman had to be as anxious as they were to catch the person who was responsible. Until he was behind bars, none of them, including Veronica, was safe.

"I didn't mention this to Miriam," Nick continued, "but I'm sure Cullen won't mind if Veronica stays here at the ranch with us."

That put even more hope in Hallie's eyes. "Yes, please ask him. I'm not sure if Veronica will take him up on it, but it'll be good for her to have options."

The woman's other option would be a safe house. Which would be good, too. Nick doubted Veronica would insist on going back alone to her place. Not after everything she'd been through there.

Nick's phone rang, the sound shooting through the room, and he answered it right away when he saw who was calling.

Ty.

Finally. Nick had left the man plenty of messages, so it was about damn time he got back to him.

"Don't bust my chops about not calling you back sooner," Ty grumbled right off the bat. "I've been at work, and I'm not allowed to make personal calls. You said in the messages you left that it was important. Did you find who killed Kelsey?" He tacked that on before Nick could speak.

"No, but I'm working on it." Nick put the call on speaker so that Hallie could hear. And so he could record it. "That's why I need to talk to both you and Lamar Travers."

"Lamar?" Ty repeated. "Wouldn't be surprised if he dodged your calls. He doesn't care much for cops."

That probably had something to do with the man's involvement in the militia. "You know where he is?" Nick asked.

"Not really. Last I heard, he was doing some ranch work. But I got his number." The one Ty rattled off was the same one that had come up when Nick had run a background check on the man.

"When's the last time you saw Lamar?" Nick asked.

Ty made a sound to indicate he was giving that some thought. "It was months ago. Like maybe right after the militia got raided. Look, it's not like we were ever close or anything. The only reason I knew him was because he's Kelsey's cousin." Ty paused. "You think Lamar killed her?"

Nick dodged that particular question. "I just need to talk to him."

"Talk like that coming from a lawman makes me think Lamar's a suspect in her death," Ty pointed out.

"Do you think he could have killed her?" Nick came out and asked.

"I don't know," Ty said after another long pause. "Lamar was into stuff. Bad stuff," he said with emphasis. "I mean, those Brothers of Freedom boys were stockpiling guns, and they had those babies they were gonna sell."

And that brought Nick right to a subject he wanted to discuss. "Did Kelsey ever say anything about selling her baby to the militia or to anyone else?"

"She never said nothing like that to me," Ty spat out fast. "I already told you I didn't know about the kid until after she'd already had it." Ty groaned. "Look, man, I just want you to arrest whoever killed her. Kelsey deserves that."

"Then help me ID the person and make sure he pays," Nick said. "Think back to around the time the baby was born. Seven months ago. Did you hear any talk whatsoever about babies being stolen or sold?"

"Stolen?" Ty blurted out. "You think somebody could have stolen Kelsey's kid?"

"It's possible." Nick settled for saying that. And he left it at that.

Ty cursed. "And you think Lamar could have done that? You believe Lamar could have taken that baby?"

"That's what I need to find out. Would Lamar have done something like that? Would Kelsey have given him the baby to sell?"

This time, Ty's hesitation was long enough that it had Nick concerned that the man wasn't going to answer. "Maybe," Ty finally said. "If Kelsey was hurtin' real bad for money, she might have done it. And Lamar might have helped her get the kid to the Brothers of Freedom."

Bingo. That would tie everything up into a neat little bow. Except for one thing. It still didn't tell them the identity of David's father, and Nick believed that was a critical piece of this puzzle.

"Who were Kelsey's other lovers when she was seeing you?" Nick asked the man. "And I know there were others," he added in a snap. "I need names."

Ty groaned. "You don't believe in not speaking ill of the dead, do you?"

"Not when it can get the dead the justice they deserve," Nick fired back. "Names," he pressed.

Ty's next groan was a lot louder. "Well, she wasn't hooking up with Lamar if that's what you're thinking. He's her cousin, and Kelsey didn't play that way. But I did hear talk about her maybe doing a cop. Or one of the guys who busted the militia. I figured it was just that—talk. Kelsey wasn't exactly squeaky clean, and I couldn't see her burning up the sheets with a badge."

That's exactly what she'd done though. Nick believed Steve's confession about the two of them having an affair. And wasn't it interesting that there was gossip about it? Too bad that gossip hadn't made it back to Nick or the ATF. If it had, Nick would have already had Steve hauled in for questioning, and Nick sure as hell wouldn't have allowed him to have any part in the militia raid.

Nick looked up at Hallie to see how she was dealing with everything she was hearing from Ty. Of course, she was hanging on every word. Along with agonizing about it, no doubt. Because if either Ty or Steve was David's father, they might try to stop the adoption that was already in progress.

"Any other lovers you know about?" Nick prompted when the man didn't say anything for several long moments.

"Maybe. People like to hear themselves talk. Like I said, Kelsey wasn't squeaky, and she liked sex."

Nick didn't give up. He kept pressing Ty. "Is there any talk that she had been with anybody in the militia?"

"I didn't hear anything, but that's probably where Lamar can help. Look, man, I gotta go, but I'll put out some feelers and see if I can track down Lamar for you."

He didn't try to stop Ty when the man blurted out a quick goodbye and ended the call. Nick figured he'd scraped out everything he was going to get, and now he had to decide if Ty had been telling the truth. *The whole truth.*

"I see this going two ways," Hallie remarked as she pushed the strands of hair off the side of her face. "Either Ty really will try to get in touch with Lamar in the hopes that it'll get you off his back. Or Ty already knows where Lamar is and doesn't want us talking to him."

Nick was in complete agreement. "Lamar might be able to shed more light on what Ty did or didn't say. Like that maybe Ty knew all along about Kelsey's baby and that he was the one who gave David to the militia."

"And by pressing us to find Kelsey's killer," Hallie added, "Ty could perhaps hope to make himself look innocent." She paused. "He might want that because he could have been the one to murder her."

There was indeed motive for Ty doing just that. If Kelsey had been making noise about contacting the ATF, specifically Hallie and him, about the black market baby ring. Of course, that motive hinged on Ty having had some part in selling or giving David to the militia.

"We need to do more digging on Ty," Nick concluded, "and I want to get him in for a formal interview."

He took out his phone to get the process started on arranging the interview, but it rang before he could make the call. Nick saw Cullen's name on the screen.

"There's a problem," Cullen said the moment Nick answered.

Nick's stomach went to his knees. "What's wrong?"

"Someone just set off one of the motion detectors by the back fence," Cullen replied. "I've sent ranch hands to intercept, but whoever it is, he's making his way to the house. Have Hallie and David take cover *now*."

Chapter Nine

Even though Nick hadn't put his brother's call on speaker, Hallie had no trouble hearing the warning. And she started running. She had to get to David now and take him somewhere safe.

Nick ran right along with her, and he didn't try to tell her that this was probably nothing. No attempts to minimize the threat. Like Hallie, he knew the danger was real and that someone could be trying to take David. Someone who would kill Nick and her to do that.

Thankfully, Cullen had put David and her in a guest room on the bottom floor so Hallie didn't have to deal with the stairs. Still, the place was sprawling, and it seemed to take an eternity to thread her way through the connecting halls and to the bedroom. David was there in his crib, right where she'd left him just minutes earlier, and he was safe.

Hallie intended for him to stay that way.

She scooped him up, which caused him to wake up and start fussing, but Hallie pressed him against her and rocked gently while she sank on the floor in the corner.

It was as far away from the windows as she could get. Which didn't seem far enough. She needed distance between David and the possible gunman. Even though the curtains were drawn, she didn't want to risk being in the line of fire in case the intruder knew which room they were in. If the intruder pinpointed their location, he could try to shoot into the house, just as the gunman had done at Nick's.

"The bathroom has windows with the block glass," she muttered to Nick. That's why she'd stayed in the bedroom. "I didn't want the gunman to see us moving around in there." Plus the glass might not be shatter-proof, especially if a bullet went flying through it.

He nodded, drew his gun and put his phone on speaker. "Are there security cameras that can pick up the intruder?" Nick asked Cullen.

"There are, but I can't see the guy from any of the angles. Not yet anyway. But he set off the motion detector in sector six. You can use your phone to take a look at exactly where that is, but there's no audio." Cullen rattled off the app and access code for Nick to do that. "Leigh's already on the way. Once she gets here, I'm going out to try to get a look at this idiot for myself."

"I need a look, too," Nick insisted. "He could be one of our suspects."

Hallie's mind hadn't worked around to that possibility yet. She was having to fight through the fear that was spiking to the point of making her panic. That wouldn't help David, so she forced herself to level out and take several deep breaths. It worked, some. It worked better for David since he put his head on her shoulder and thankfully went back to sleep.

"The house is locked up tight," Cullen added a moment later. "If you have to go out, plug in the code on the app first or it'll cause the alarms to go off."

Hallie knew those instructions were for Nick, not her. She'd be staying inside with David, but Nick might decide to act on his "I need a look, too," and go outside to have a showdown.

Part of her welcomed that and wanted to be in on it.

She wanted to be involved in taking down the person who'd already caused her so many nightmares. But she didn't want Nick, Cullen or anyone else out there where they could be gunned down. Maybe, just maybe, it wouldn't take Leigh long to arrive, and she'd come with plenty of her deputies. That way, if this snake tried to run, there'd be plenty of badges to chase him down.

Her hands were trembling, but Nick's were steady as a rock when he ended the call with his brother and began to work his way through the app to bring up the security cameras. When he finally got through, he eased down next to her, keeping his gun away from David but holding his phone so that she could see the screen.

And what she saw was nothing.

Well, no people anyway. It was one of the many fences on the Triple R Ranch. Nick scrolled through the other camera feeds and stopped on the one identified as sector six.

Still nothing.

It was more pasture, fences and some trees. However, when he moved just one camera over, Hallie could see two armed men.

"They're Cullen's ranch hands," Nick said quickly before the panic could slam into her again.

They were indeed dressed like cowboys, and they were firing glances all around them. No doubt looking for the person who'd set off that motion detector. It was eerie watching them move through the night and the shadows while hearing nothing but the soft static from the camera feed.

"There are so many places to hide," she muttered as Nick scanned past more trees and even some horses.

If the intruder was smart, he would have known he'd likely trigger the security system and had probably hit the ground running. Heading straight for cover. If so, he could be anywhere on the ranch right now. Those two ranch hands could be walking right into the line of fire. Or even past him if the person had managed to find a good place to hide. Then, he could wait for an opening to get to the house.

Since the person who'd broken into her house had managed to disarm the security system, she had to consider that it could happen again. A jammer could shut off the alarms, and they might not even know the person was inside. Of course, that person would then have to make his way through the maze of rooms in the house, but if he continued to stay quiet and keep out of sight, he might manage to get to them.

Nick's phone dinged, and because her nerves were right there at the surface, Hallie had to bite back a gasp. When she focused, she saw Cullen's brief text pop onto the screen.

Check sector four on the security app, Cullen texted. I'm heading out now to look for this SOB.

She held her breath as Nick went to the sector four camera, and Hallie silently cursed when she still didn't see anyone. She'd wanted to get a look at the guy's face because once they knew who he was, then they'd know why these attacks were happening. Well, maybe they would. Or it was possible one of their suspects had sent a hired gun.

"There," Nick said, tapping the far edge of the screen.

Hallie picked through the darkness and finally saw something. It was just a blur of motion. But something or someone had definitely moved behind one of the large pecan trees.

Nick shifted the camera angle again, and she spotted two men. More ranch hands, no doubt, since they weren't trying to hide or evade. Just the opposite. They were moving straight toward where she'd seen that blur.

The sound stopped them.

Her breath stalled in her lungs. Because she knew exactly what it was.

A gunshot.

Oh, mercy. Someone was shooting. Hallie heard

it loud and clear even though the sound hadn't come through the camera feed. And it meant the gunman was close to the house. The ranch was so big that had he still been by the back fence, the blast wouldn't have been as loud.

The two ranch hands dropped to the ground, scrambling behind the cover of another tree, but she couldn't tell if one of them had been hit. She prayed they hadn't been and that they'd be able to return fire and protect themselves.

Hallie relaxed just a little when she heard the sound of the approaching police sirens. Leigh and her deputies, no doubt. If this was the same gunman who'd shot up Nick's house, then the sirens might cause him to run again. This time though, there were ranch hands and Cullen ready to chase him down. Maybe, just maybe, they'd catch him, too.

She continued to watch the screen, looking for the person who'd darted behind that tree. And Hallie finally got a glimpse of him. It was definitely a man, but his dark clothes blended with the night, and he had a ski mask covering his face. If this was one of their suspects, she had no idea which one since they all had similar builds.

Every muscle in her body tightened when she saw the gunman take aim again, and he fired.

Nick cursed under his breath. No doubt because he had to wonder if that shot had hit his brother or one of the ranch hands.

The sound of hurried footsteps had Nick pivoting in the direction of the doorway, but he lowered his gun when Leigh called out. "It's me," she said, and rushed in. Not alone though. There was a female deputy with her.

Leigh glanced at them and at the screen of Nick's phone. "Cullen's out there?" she asked.

Nick nodded. "Yeah."

Leigh was a cop, but she was also in love with the man who could be in grave danger, and that fear instantly showed on her face. "I'm going out there, too," Leigh insisted.

"So am I," Nick told her.

That gave Hallie another jolt of the panic that she'd been trying to stave off. Sweet heaven, she wanted him inside and away from the shooter, but she knew he wouldn't stay put with his brother and the hands in the line of fire. Besides, he might be the one to stop this monster.

"Can your deputy stay with Hallie and the baby?" Nick asked Leigh.

Leigh nodded and glanced at Hallie before she tipped her head to the deputy. "This is Deputy Dawn Farley. She's good, and she'll protect you."

Hallie didn't doubt that. No way would Nick have asked for this arrangement if he hadn't known that David and she would be safe. Well, as safe as they could be considering gunshots could be fired into the house.

"You can keep watch on the security cameras," Nick

explained, handing Hallie his phone. "Leigh and I can use hers to locate Cullen and the gunman."

Hallie took the phone and held Nick's gaze for a few precious seconds. "Be careful."

"I will." He said it like a promise, but she knew he'd do everything to end this danger. Even if it put him at risk.

Leigh and Nick hurried out of the room, and Dawn eased down on the floor next to Hallie. "He's a cute kid," she murmured, glancing at David.

Hallie muttered a thanks, but she couldn't keep up any small talk. Not when she was so worried about Nick and the others. She kept her attention pinned to the phone screen, scanning through the sectors as Nick had done. Beside her, the deputy did the same while volleying glances at the door and the window. She was staying vigilant in case the gunman brought this attack any closer.

Hallie spotted Leigh and Nick in the sector nearest the house, and she saw that Leigh was indeed using her phone while Nick and she moved at a clipped pace over the ranch grounds. Hallie continued to follow them on the screen.

And she heard the shot.

It was another powerful blast that tore through the air, and it hadn't come from Nick or Leigh. It also hadn't come from the same direction as the other shots. This one sounded closer.

The gunman was moving in, trying to get to them.

Nick and Leigh ducked, but they didn't stay put. They continued to move, causing Hallie to switch to the camera of the next sector on the security grid. She quickly picked them up, and she could have sworn her heart skipped a couple of beats when there was another gunshot. Then, another.

Hallie groaned. There was a gunfight going on, one that'd started because someone wanted to get to David, and there was nothing she could do but sit there and watch. Worse, even with Leigh, Cullen and Nick putting their lives on the line, they might not be able to stop the intruder from getting inside. If that happened, Hallie would fight and do whatever it took to keep this monster away from her son.

The seconds crawled by, bleeding into minutes. Minutes that seemed to take an eternity. Her hand was trembling when Hallie switched the camera to continue following Leigh and Nick, and the tightness in her chest eased a little when she saw Cullen meet up with them. Two of the ranch hands were with him, and none of them appeared to be hurt. Thank God. Maybe it would stay that way.

Nick and the others had a brief conversation, one that Hallie wished she could hear, but then Nick looked up at the camera. Looking at her, Hallie realized. Nick took Leigh's phone, lifting it so she could see, and he used it to call his own phone that she was holding. The moment she saw Leigh's name on the screen, Hallie hit answer so that the ringing wouldn't wake up David.

"Are you all right?" Hallie blurted out, trying to keep her voice at a whisper. Hard to do with the emotions whipping through her.

"Fine. We're all fine. Cullen or one of the hands shot him. The man who was firing those shots is dead."

Dead. Hallie had never thought hearing that word would give her any relief. But it did. Mercy, did it. The relief relaxed all the tight muscles in her body.

"Who is he?" Hallie asked. "Steve? Ty—"

"We're not sure," Nick interrupted, "and Leigh doesn't want any of us touching the body to remove the mask because the kill shot was to the head."

Which could mean there was a lot of damage to the face. They might have to get an ID from fingerprints. Still, since they had a body, they would eventually be able to figure out who he was.

Nick paused. "There was a second man."

Hallie choked back a gasp. "What do you mean?" There was so much breath in her voice that it hardly had any sound.

"The ranch hands said they spotted two men. *Two.* One who fired shots and a second one who stayed near the back fence. They didn't see him with a gun, but he ran and got away." Nick groaned and ground out some profanity. "I'm sorry, Hallie, but this might not be over."

NICK SAT ON the floor with David and played blocks with the baby. Except *played* probably wasn't the right word for what they were doing. Nick stacked up the large

FREE BOOKS GIVEAWAY

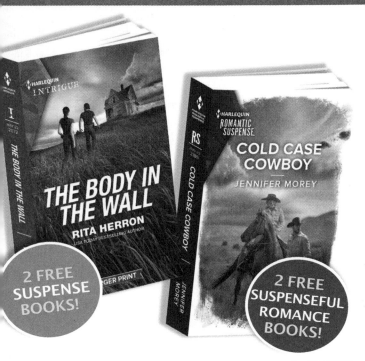

2 FREE SUSPENSE BOOKS!

2 FREE SUSPENSEFUL ROMANCE BOOKS!

GET UP TO FOUR FREE BOOKS & TWO FREE GIFTS WORTH OVER $20!

We pay for everything!

See Details Inside

YOU pick your books –
WE pay for everything.
You get up to FOUR New Books and
TWO Mystery Gifts...absolutely FREE!

Dear Reader,

I am writing to announce the launch of a huge **FREE BOOK GIVEAWAY**... and to let you know that YOU are entitled to choose up to FOUR fantastic books that WE pay for.

Try **Harlequin® Romantic Suspense** books featuring heart-racing page-turners with unexpected plot twists and irresistible chemistry that will keep you guessing to the very end.

Try **Harlequin Intrigue® Larger-Print** books featuring action-packed stories that will keep you on the edge of your seat. Solve the crime and deliver justice at all costs.

Or TRY BOTH!

In return, we ask just one favor: Would you please participate in our brief Reader Survey? We'd love to hear from you.

This FREE BOOKS GIVEAWAY means that your introductory shipment is completely free, <u>even the shipping</u>! If you decide to continue, you can look forward to curated monthly shipments of brand-new books from your selected series, always at a discount off the cover price! <u>Plus you can cancel any time</u>. Who could pass up a deal like that?

Sincerely

Pam Powers

Pam Powers
For Harlequin Reader Service

Complete the survey below and return it today to receive up to 4 FREE BOOKS and FREE GIFTS guaranteed!

FREE BOOKS GIVEAWAY
Reader Survey

1
Do you prefer stories with suspensful storylines?

◯ YES ◯ NO

2
Do you share your favorite books with friends?

◯ YES ◯ NO

3
Do you often choose to read instead of watching TV?

◯ YES ◯ NO

YES! Please send me my Free Rewards, consisting of **2 Free Books from each series I select** and **Free Mystery Gifts**. I understand that I am under no obligation to buy anything, no purchase necessary see terms and conditions for details.

❏ **Harlequin® Romantic Suspense** (240/340 HDL GRNT)
❏ **Harlequin Intrigue® Larger-Print** (199/399 HDL GRNT)
❏ **Try Both** (240/340 & 199/399 HDL GRN5)

FIRST NAME | LAST NAME

ADDRESS

APT.# | CITY

STATE/PROV. | ZIP/POSTAL CODE

EMAIL ❏ Please check this box if you would like to receive newsletters and promotional emails from Harlequin Enterprises ULC and its affiliates. You can unsubscribe anytime.

HARLEQUIN® Reader Service — Terms and Conditions:

plastic blocks, and while giggling as if it was the most fun game ever, David knocked them down.

The boy's laughter definitely helped Nick with the fatigue he was feeling from yet another sleepless night and plenty of spent adrenaline. Maybe it'd do the same for Hallie once she finished her shower. The shower might help as well, though Nick had had to talk her into taking it while he watched the baby. He wasn't sure if Hallie was just uncertain about his babysitting skills or if she was still too worried to have David out of her sight.

Nick totally got the "out of her sight" thing. Once again, shots had been fired around the baby, and while these bullets hadn't come close to hitting the house, there'd been the threat of just that happening.

However, the worst threat came from the second man the hands had spotted during the latest attack. Every now and then, someone would sneak onto the ranch to try to steal something, but Nick doubted that was the case here. No. There was someone else out there who could come after them again. Well, unless the second man was a hired gun. If that was the case, then maybe the death of his comrade had spooked him and the guy would just go away.

But Nick figured they weren't going to get that lucky.

So, they had to prepare not only for another attempt on their lives but also continue to dig hard to get to the bottom of why someone had tried to kill them.

Once Hallie had showered and was dressed, they'd

refocus on the investigation into the attack. Something they'd done well past midnight and then picked up again once David had had his breakfast. It was still early, going on ten, so they'd have more time to try to pick through the camera feed and try to find the second man. If they could just get a hint of his face, they might know who he was. Then, they could possibly be able to tell if he was a hired gun. Or if he'd been one who'd done the hiring.

They'd soon know the identity of the dead gunman, too. There had been no ID on the man so they'd had no help there. Added to that, Dark River didn't have its own medical examiner. It was too small of a town for that. But the county ME had finally gotten a team out to the ranch at midnight, and the body had been transported to the morgue.

The one thing the ME had confirmed on scene was there was indeed damage to the gunman's face. Plenty of it. In fact, so much that it made a visual ID impossible. That would slow down the ID process, but maybe the delay wouldn't be too long. If someone hadn't already gotten started on examining the body, that would soon happen. Then, Nick would know if it was Steve, Darius, Ty, Lamar or someone else.

Hell.

That ate away at him, and the only thing that saved Nick from cursing was David giggling again. Because that laughter kept him from sinking into a nasty dark mood, he gave him a kiss on his forehead. A raspberry kiss that had David cackling.

Since Hallie had left the bathroom door ajar, he heard when she turned off the water in the shower. He heard the soft click as she opened the shower door, too. Apparently, the air circulation was darn good because he even caught a whiff of the soap she'd used. Lavender. It wasn't normally a scent he associated with sex, but his mind immediately latched on to an image of Hallie stepping from the shower.

She'd be wet and warm.

And naked, of course.

It didn't matter that Nick had never actually seen her without her clothes, but his imagination was pretty good when it came to Hallie, and his body was filling in the blanks. Blanks that he didn't have to keep filling in when she finally stepped into the room.

She wasn't naked now, but it was close enough for him to fill in more blanks. She was wearing a short white terry-cloth bathrobe that hit her midthigh. And yeah, she was still wet. Her face was flushed and damp, and when she looked at him, Nick could have sworn the earth tipped just a little.

Man, he had it bad for her.

She opened her mouth to say something but smiled instead when she saw him playing with David. It didn't last though. She quickly shook her head.

"Sorry," Hallie said. "I don't want you to think I'm going all goo-goo eyed over you being with David."

It took Nick a moment to work his way through what she meant. Or at least he thought he knew what she was getting at. Hallie didn't want him to believe she was seeing him as daddy material.

"It's okay," he assured her. "The only goo-goo eyes I saw was from a mother who obviously loves her son. Though I'd rather it not get around that I use words like goo-goo eyes," he added with a wink.

She laughed, and man, it was just as mood lifting as David's. Hallie went to them, sinking to the floor. The robe was loose, and when it shifted, he got a peek at the top of her right breast.

So much for giving up on the lust.

"Could you please put a new dressing on my arm?" she asked, taking a wrapped bandage from the pocket of the robe. "I've already managed to put on antiseptic cream," she explained, "but I can't do the bandage myself."

He certainly hadn't forgotten that Hallie had been injured by a bullet and had stitches, but with everything else going on, Nick hadn't remembered to ask her if she was in pain. That was yet another reason for him to shove this whole lust thing aside. Hallie was hurt, and that was a reminder that he needed to focus on stopping another attack so that she wouldn't be hurt again.

"The stitches are at an angle that's hard for me to reach, and I don't want to get the bandage adhesive on the wound," she continued, easing down the shoulder of the robe several more inches to expose her arm.

The wound didn't look bad, only a couple of stitches, but it was still a gut punch to see it, and it took care of the renewed lust over seeing a good portion of her breast. Nick replaced the bandage as fast, and as gently, as he could, and she slid the robe back in place.

"Thanks," she muttered. There was something in her tone, a weariness, that had him meeting her eye to eye. "I'm okay," Hallie assured him.

He doubted she could read his mind, but she must have seen the guilt and regret on his face. Nick wished he could have stopped her from being hurt.

"I see David has taught you his favorite game?" Hallie remarked. She scooped up the baby and kissed him.

Nick made a sound of agreement. "I think he has a future as a demolitions expert."

David must have thought that was a fine joke because he giggled, causing Hallie to smile again. There was a lot of love going on between them, and it made Nick want to dig in and try harder to keep them safe. It made him thankful, too, that Hallie had claimed this little boy. David had had a rocky start, but he was obviously in loving hands now.

His phone rang, and because Nick had been expecting the call from Leigh, he answered it right away. Since Hallie would no doubt want to hear as well, he put the call on speaker.

"The ME just confirmed the ID on the body," Leigh immediately said. "It's Lamar Travers."

For just a moment, Nick was stunned. Though he shouldn't have been. Lamar had been on their list of suspects, and the man had ties to both the militia and to Kelsey. That, in turn, meant Lamar had ties to Hallie, David and him. But Nick's shocked reaction was more because he still wasn't sure why Lamar had tried to kill them.

"Lamar," Hallie repeated in a whisper. She groaned, probably because they hadn't gotten the chance to interrogate the man. And now they never would.

"The ME office did a thorough search, but there was no ID on the body," Leigh went on. "No personal effects of any kind. There weren't even any prints on the gun because Lamar was wearing latex gloves."

Now, that was interesting, and judging from the way Hallie's eyebrow rose, she thought so, too. Most criminals didn't wear gloves unless they were planning on coming in direct contact with someone or something where they might leave DNA or trace evidence. Maybe that meant Lamar had intended to try to break into the house and had fired shots only because the ranch hands had intercepted him.

"We might be able to get something off the gun itself," Leigh went on a moment later, "but I'm betting it was something from his time in the militia. They had a lot of weapons stockpiled."

True, and Nick was betting the same thing. "Any idea how Lamar got to the ranch?"

"None," Leigh answered without hesitation. "Cullen sent out nearly a dozen ranch hands to comb the old ranch trails, especially the one near the fence where someone first triggered the motion detector, and they came up with zilch. It's possible Lamar came to the ranch with the second man who was spotted, and when the man ran, he left in the vehicle they'd used to drive here."

Yeah, that theory would work for Nick. It also meant the second man had driven away with potential evidence that would give them answers as to Lamar's specific motive. Maybe that second man was also another of their suspects?

"Did anyone see any tire tracks near the fence?" Nick asked.

"No, it's rocky back there, and there weren't any visible impressions," Leigh answered, dashing his hopes about the CSIs being able to get any info from that.

"I want Lubbock PD to show Lamar's picture to Veronica," Nick said. "She might recognize him as the man who attacked her."

"I'll have to check with her doctors first," Leigh explained. "I'm not sure how they'd feel about approaching her again since they didn't want us to push for anything that might give her false memories."

Nick understood that. He wanted Veronica's recollections to be the real deal, but he was hoping they could spur that "real deal" along. It was a long shot, but it would help Nick if he knew just how involved Lamar was in all of this. It was possible that Lamar had orchestrated and carried out all of it and the man who ran was simply a lackey. If so, the guy might not be a threat. However, he'd darn sure be able to close out this investigation. Well, some parts of it anyway by confirming Lamar's involvement, but Lamar might not have informed a hired gun of his motive.

"There's something else," Leigh went on several moments later. "Maybe connected, maybe not. One of my deputies arrested Ty Levine late last night."

"What?" Nick and Hallie asked in unison. "Arrested him for what?" Nick asked.

"He was drunk and got into a fight at the Hitching Post. He and another customer got into it, and Ty threw some punches."

The Hitching Post was a bar in town, miles from the ranch, but it was also miles from Ty's home in Lubbock.

"Did he say why he was in Dark River?" Nick asked.

"He claims he was supposed to meet a woman who didn't show, but he wasn't sober enough to remember the woman's name," Leigh said with loads of skepticism. "Anyway, I've still got him in custody, and I thought you might want to have a chat with him before I let him go."

"You bet I do," Nick answered, and Hallie made a quick sound of agreement. "How long can you hold him?"

"Until his bail hearing in about two hours. Longer, if he doesn't make bail. I'll go ahead and send someone to follow you into town. Just get with Cullen and let him know when you'll be leaving."

"Will do," Nick assured her.

"I'm going with you," Hallie said the moment Nick ended the call. She rose from the floor, scooping up David and heading to the closet. No doubt so she could start getting dressed. "I can ask Rosa to stay with David again."

No way would Nick talk her out of this, and he didn't want to do that anyway. Hallie had been a good interrogator, and she might be able to get something from Ty they could use. Or trick him into confessing that he was the second man the ranch hands had spotted.

Nick started to text Leigh to get a copy of the incident report for Ty's arrest, but before he could do that, his phone rang.

"It's Miriam," he said to Hallie.

She'd just taken a blue summer top and jeans from the closet, but Hallie turned around to face him as he put the call on speaker.

"I heard about the trouble at your brother's ranch," Miriam stated. "Are you all okay?"

"Yeah. I'm guessing you also know the shooter was Lamar and that he's dead?"

"Yes, I just read the prelim report on that. I'd planned on bringing Lamar in for questioning in regards to Kelsey's death. And no, I don't have anything specific on him," Miriam added before Nick could ask. "I just wanted a chat with him to find out if he knew something."

"Hallie and I are about to have a chat with Ty Levine. If he tells us anything of interest, I'll let you know."

"Levine," Miriam repeated. "Why are you questioning him?"

"He was arrested for a bar fight here in Dark River. *Here, last night.*" Nick emphasized the words so that Miriam would understand the timing of it.

"Yes, I'll be very interested to hear what he has to say about that," Miriam assured him. Then, she paused. Nick also heard her take a deep breath. "The DNA sample I took from David doesn't match the one taken shortly after the militia raid."

She waited a couple of seconds, no doubt to give Nick some time to absorb that. But Hallie was the one who really needed those seconds. She certainly wasn't smiling now, and the nerves were right there at the surface— again. Because this was a threat of a different kind but still a threat.

"Someone tampered with the DNA," Nick finally said to Miriam. "Not on your end with the latest test," he added. "The tampering would have happened right after David was taken into custody at the militia compound."

"That's my guess, too, and it's why I'm running the sample I took through the databases again." Miriam muttered something he didn't catch, but it was accompanied by another long, heavy breath. "Look, you should try to steel up Hallie for this because we might get a match."

And there it was—the threat, all spelled out for them.

A match was a strong possibility, especially if David's father was Steve or Darius. Both would be in the system. Steve because he was a former ATF agent and Darius because he had a criminal record. Ty might not be in the databases though, and Nick made a mental note to try to get a DNA sample from him. Ty would have to give it voluntarily unless Nick could manage a warrant. With what little evidence he had, getting it would be a long shot.

Hopefully, the warrant would come through on Steve's financials, and maybe there'd be some flags if the man was truly guilty. Then again, a former agent might know how to hide any transactions that would prove he'd done something wrong.

Hallie used the house phone to call Rosa, and even though Nick could only hear Hallie's side of the conversation, he could tell that Rosa had said she'd be pleased to take care of David. Nick took that one step further. After he ended the call with Miriam, he texted Cullen, asking him for not only the armed ranch hands to escort them into town but also for beefed up security around the house while Hallie and he were gone. Things were already beefed up, but it wouldn't hurt to have a few more of the hands nearby in case something went wrong. Ditto for adding some backup for the deputy Leigh was sending out to follow them into town.

"I can watch David while you get dressed," Nick told

Hallie when he saw the baby trying to grab the shoes that she'd also taken from the closet.

When he went to them, David reached right out for him, and the baby began to babble as if he had a story to tell. Nick couldn't help but smile, and he extended the smile to Hallie after she gave him another of those looks. The look that said she didn't want him playing daddy. He wasn't. But Nick was finding himself more and more at ease with the baby.

More and more stressed, too.

Because protecting David was now at the top of his list.

He certainly intended to keep Hallie safe, too, but she was an adult. A former ATF agent. And she had self-defense and firearms training. David was not only vulnerable, it was highly likely that he was the main target of this SOB who'd already come after him not once but three times now. Three was a pattern, and that meant if the SOB was alive, he'd continue to try to get the baby.

Hallie carried her clothes into the bathroom to get dressed so Nick got back on the floor to entertain David with the blocks. At the same time, he called Miriam and asked her to have someone take Lamar's DMV photo to show Veronica. However, before he could do that, Rosa stepped into the doorway.

"There's a visitor," the woman said. "The ranch hands stopped her from coming to the door, but she's insisting on seeing Hallie."

She must have heard because she hurried out of the bathroom. "Who is it?" she asked.

Rosa was literally wringing her hands, and everything about her body language said there was trouble. Bracing himself for it, Nick picked up David and stood.

"Her name is Jennifer Lowe," Rosa answered. "She's from Child Protective Services." The woman's voice cracked. "And she says she's here to take David."

Chapter Ten

Hallie had dealt with a lot of slams of adrenaline over the past forty-eight hours, but this one was the worst. Because losing David would be harder than going through another attack.

"She can't take him," Hallie managed to say. Her voice was weak. Spineless. It disgusted her so she did something about that. She let the fresh adrenaline fuel her determination. "CPS won't take him," she amended.

"No, they won't," Nick agreed. "I'll handle this."

Since Nick had a badge, it would be easy for Hallie to hand over that duty to him, but David was her child. And she needed to do this herself.

"Could you please watch David for me?" Hallie asked Rosa.

"Of course," the woman quickly agreed. She went and took David from Hallie's arms. "Ms. Lowe is in her car that's parked in front of the house, but if you tell the hands who are keeping an eye on her, they'll escort her in."

Hallie didn't especially want the social worker in the

house, but she couldn't risk carrying on a conversation with her outside. Not with that second "person of interest" still at large. With all the security, it would be hard for that person to sneak onto the grounds, but it wasn't impossible. The person could go into sniper mode and try to take shots at them.

While she walked to the front of the house—with Nick right beside her—Hallie tamped down her fear over losing her child and considered how best to approach this. If she emphasized there'd been an attack just the night before, Ms. Lowe might consider it proof that David needed to be removed.

Of course, it was highly likely that the social worker was already aware of what was going on or she wouldn't have come here. So, Hallie would just need to convince her that taking David wouldn't be in the best interest of the child. And it wasn't. Hallie believed that because no one would lay down their lives to protect David as Nick and she would do. Cullen and Leigh as well.

Nick made it to the front door ahead of her, but instead of opening it, he made a call. To Child Protective Services, she realized. And he verified that they had indeed sent out a Ms. Lowe to the ranch. He then asked for a photo of the woman. A precaution that Hallie was very glad he was taking. When the photo loaded on his screen, he peered out the window to the woman who was pacing by a black car.

"It's her," Nick said, verifying the woman's identity. He ended the call with CPS and disarmed the security system so he could open the door and motion to the hands to let the woman in. Ms. Lowe wore a simple beige skirt and white top, and she had her dark auburn hair pulled up. She was tall, willowy thin. And clearly riled. Probably because the hands had "detained" her.

"I'm guessing you think it's necessary to have these armed men stand guard over someone with CPS credentials?" the woman snarled, aiming that complaint at Hallie.

"I do," Hallie answered, her tone a cool contrast to Ms. Lowe's heated one. "As you know, someone has attempted to kidnap David. Credentials are easy to fake. Your office just verified that you are who you say you are."

The woman's shoulders stiffened, but Hallie didn't think the reaction was caused by more anger. Maybe it was finally getting through to Ms. Lowe that there was a huge security issue, and that Nick and she were taking these steps because they were vital to keeping the baby safe.

Ms. Lowe finally gave a crisp nod and came inside the house when Hallie and Nick stepped back. "I need you to bring David to me," the woman insisted. "His foster mother is hospitalized, and there is no authority for him to be here with you."

"But there is." Nick spoke up. He'd already scrolled through something on his phone, and he showed it to the woman. "That's an order placing David in protective custody of Leigh Mercer, the sheriff of Dark River.

This is her home, and it's where she's keeping David. Sheriff Mercer also named me, Hallie and my brother, Cullen, as co-providers of David's protection."

Hallie hadn't known that Leigh had finalized the order, but she was beyond thankful for it. Thankful, too, that it had extended to Nick and her. Hallie suspected Leigh had added Cullen's name because the ranch belonged to him and also because he worked mostly from home. Cullen was more likely to be in residence than Leigh was.

Ms. Lowe took the phone and spent several minutes reading the document. "Why hasn't CPS received this?"

"They should have by now," Nick answered. "You could have probably saved yourself a trip out here if you'd checked first."

Oh, the woman didn't like that, and her eyes narrowed. Hallie didn't know if it was because she didn't like Nick dressing her down or if she thought her authority had been usurped. Which it had been.

"Protective custody orders can be challenged," the woman snapped.

Again, Hallie kept her tone calm and level. "Certainly you're aware that David's at risk," Hallie explained. "*You* would be at risk if you tried to drive out of here with him. You could be killed on the way back to CPS, and David could be kidnapped."

Mercy, it ate away at her to even speak those words aloud. Because they were true. Not just for Ms. Lowe but for anyone else who might get in the attacker's way.

"You could challenge the protective custody order," Hallie continued while the woman stared at her, "but knowing the extreme threat to David's safety, why would you?"

"Because your adoption might not go through," Ms. Lowe answered in a snap. She sighed and seemed to take the anger down a couple of notches. "And because David's biological father might come forward to claim him."

Everything inside Hallie went still. "And why do you think he'll come forward after all this time?"

Ms. Lowe took a deep breath. "I got an email from someone claiming to be his father, and he indicated he'd be seeking custody of him."

"Who and when?" Nick demanded before Hallie could get the words out.

The woman seemed to hesitate about giving them that kind of info, but after several long moments, she answered. "I got the email about two hours ago."

Two hours. Long after Lamar had been killed. And it was proof that someone was out there still pulling strings. Or trying to pull them anyway. Maybe the second man who'd come onto the ranch. Maybe someone else.

"The person didn't give his name," the social worker went on. "But he insisted he could prove he was the child's father."

So, this was another of those anonymous contacts. Hallie was getting sick of them. "David's real father shouldn't have an issue giving you his name," Hallie pointed out. "Especially if he has this so-called proof and wants custody."

"In the email, he said he was afraid to try to claim David because he thought you and Agent Nick Brodie would try to kill him," Ms. Lowe explained. "He insisted you'd do anything to keep the baby."

The last bit was partly true. She would do plenty to keep him. But she wouldn't murder someone with a rightful claim to the child. However, Hallie would make sure that person was arrested if it turned out he'd had a part in Kelsey's death and the attacks.

"David's biological father would be a suspect," Nick told the social worker. "A possible *murder* suspect," he said with emphasis. "Along with perhaps being responsible for a long list of other felonies connected to the attacks. Even if this person made himself known and proved he had fathered David, there's no way you could or would just hand over the child."

Ms. Lowe certainly didn't argue with that.

"It's possible this man who contacted you did so in the hopes that you'd make it easier for him to get to David," Hallie added, taking up Nick's argument. "That's why David's staying here. If and when you get proof of David's biological father, the ATF, Lubbock PD and the Dark River sheriff will all want to question him. Until then, David isn't leaving the safety of this ranch."

The woman stayed quiet for several moments and then finally nodded. "But I'll need to speak to Sheriff

Mercer, to clarify that she or someone she designates needs to give me daily updates about David."

"She's at her office in town right now," Nick explained, "but her contact numbers are on the protective custody order. Hallie and I can give you daily updates as well."

Ms. Lowe took a little time, either processing that or deciding whether or not to push her objection. But she finally nodded. "Daily updates," she insisted. "If I don't get them, I'll be back, and I'll take David until I can verify or disprove that his biological father does indeed want custody of him."

The woman turned and walked out, but Hallie saw her cast some uneasy glances around her as she made her way back to her car. Maybe she wouldn't be making a return visit. Also, the woman would hopefully be able to confirm the email about David's father was a hoax.

"You think it's still okay for us to go to Leigh's office?" Hallie asked.

"Yeah." Nick closed the door and reset the security alarm. "We need to find out if Ty was the one who sent Ms. Lowe that email. Among other things," he added. "I want to push him hard because I know in my gut that he's holding something back."

Hallie had the same feeling, and it was the need to find out that *something* that had her keeping her goodbye to David short. That and the fact that he was clearly ready for his morning nap. If Nick and she hurried, they might finish up with Ty and make it back to the ranch before the baby even woke up.

Nick was clearly just finishing a phone conversation when Hallie stepped out of the bedroom. "Ms. Lowe has left the grounds, and two of Leigh's deputies just pulled up," he explained. "Dawn will stay here with David and Rosa, and the other deputy, Vance Pickering, will follow us into town."

Hallie made a mental note to thank Leigh for that as well. The ranch hands were obviously standing guard since they'd stopped Ms. Lowe from just driving in, but it would be good to have a deputy in the house.

As Nick and she made their way to the garage, Hallie spotted Dawn coming in through the front, and she waved to the deputy. Nick made a quick call to Cullen, to tell him what was going on, and they got into Nick's SUV that he'd parked in the massive garage. The deputy who was driving the cruiser stayed right behind them as Nick drove toward town.

With the silence, Hallie finally got a chance to try to wrap her mind around what had just happened. Having the CPS worker show up had been another scare, but now that she was working past that feeling, there was something about what Ms. Lowe had told them that stood out.

"If Ty was in custody since last night, then he probably couldn't have sent that email to CPS," Hallie pointed out.

"Maybe." Like her, Nick kept watch around them.

"But he could have scheduled it to be sent when he'd have an alibi. An alibi he could have set up by drinking and getting himself arrested. It's also possible Ty talked one of the deputies into letting him use his phone. Maybe during the one phone call he would have been allowed to make."

True, and if he'd done that, then it meant he was in on the attacks. Well, maybe. Or it was possible that Ty truly did believe he'd be killed for revealing that he was David's father.

There were no other vehicles on the rural road that led into town, but Hallie's heart rate spiked when she saw the people milling around on Main Street. Dark River was a small town, so a stranger would probably stand out. But there was still the possibility that someone might try to lie in wait, gun them down and then backtrack to the ranch to go after David.

Nick parked in front of the police station, and along with the deputy, they hurried inside. Hallie spotted Leigh right away in the doorway of her office, and the sheriff immediately motioned for them to follow her.

"I had Ty moved to an interview room," Leigh explained. "He's been read his rights and has refused an attorney, but he can also refuse to talk to you," she added as a reminder.

That might happen, but Hallie was hoping they'd get something out of the man and that this wouldn't be a wasted trip.

"Thank you for everything," Hallie told her as they reached the interview room door.

"No problem." Leigh gave Hallie's uninjured arm a gentle squeeze. "If you need anything else, just ask." She shifted her attention to Nick. "Once you're done with the chat, drop by my office and let me know so I can have him taken over to his bond hearing. If all goes as expected, he'll be out within the hour."

Hallie wished Ty could be locked up longer, at least until Nick and she had a handle on who was behind the attacks. Still, even if Ty was responsible, that didn't mean he didn't have a henchman or two to do his bidding.

Ty was seated at a gray metal table. He wasn't cuffed though, and he practically jumped to attention when they went into the room. "What are y'all doing here?" he demanded.

"Visiting you," Leigh replied, her tone as dry as west Texas dust, and she closed the door behind her when she left.

"You'd better not try to pin any other charges on me," Ty grumbled, spearing Nick with his glare. "Because I need to get home."

Without responding to that, Nick and she sat at the table. "We came to tell you that Lamar's dead," Nick stated, throwing it out there.

Hallie kept her eyes pinned to Ty, watching his reaction. His eyes widened, and the look of shock covered his face. Well, maybe it was faked shock.

"You killed him?" Ty snapped.

Nick shook his head. "He broke onto the Triple R Ranch last night. He was armed. And he was shot."

Ty shook his head, and as if his legs had gone out from under him, he dropped down into his chair. "Lamar's dead," he muttered. He scrubbed his hand over his face, said a single word of raw profanity and then repeated it.

"That's a serious reaction to a man you claimed you didn't know that well," Nick pointed out. "Is it a coincidence that you said you'd try to track him down and he's now dead?"

Again, Ty appeared stunned, and he was shaking his head as soon as Nick finished. "I didn't have anything to do with him getting shot. You said it happened last night?" He didn't wait to have that verified. "Well, I was right here. I couldn't have done it."

"Yeah, but that doesn't mean you didn't talk him into going to the ranch. Maybe to kidnap Kelsey's baby." Nick paused a heartbeat. "*Your* baby?"

Ty cursed again. "I already told you I don't know if the kid is mine, but…" Now, he stopped, groaned. "But I mighta have known Lamar a little better than I said I did. I went to a couple of meetings at the militia with him."

Hallie wasn't surprised in the least, and she jumped right on that. "Did you join?"

Ty shrugged and grumbled something under his breath that she didn't catch. "I guess I did." His gaze fired to hers. "Hey, I didn't do anything illegal. I just wanted to hang out there, and some of the guys were okay."

"Some of the guys were stockpiling illegal weapons, buying drugs and running a black market baby ring," Nick quickly reminded him. "Did you get involved with that, Ty?"

"No." He was fast to answer, but then he lowered his head. "I didn't know they had babies in the camp. I swear, I didn't."

"But?" Hallie pressed when he didn't continue.

Ty didn't say anything for several snail-crawling moments. "I didn't know about the babies," he repeated. "But after Kelsey died, Lamar mentioned that she'd told him that she was going to come clean with the ATF. Come clean with you, too," he added to Hallie.

She tried to tamp down any reaction to that, but her mind was already whirling with possibilities. One possibility anyway. That Kelsey had indeed sold David to the militia.

"Come clean about what?" Hallie asked, keeping her voice low and gentle. She didn't want Ty shutting down now, and if he realized just how high the stakes were for her, he might not want to risk saying anything that could incriminate him.

Ty shrugged again. "According to Lamar, Kelsey was going to tell you about David." He lifted his head, looked at her. "Lamar thought that Kelsey got some money for giving up David. To a good home," he hurriedly said. "Somebody in the militia told Kelsey that he'd be going to a good home, to somebody rich who wanted him enough that they'd pay big bucks for him."

And there it was. The admission that Kelsey had indeed sold her own child. Well, maybe that's what had actually happened. But it was just as possible that Lamar had lied. Or that Ty was lying now. However, if Kelsey had indeed handed over her son to the militia and then wanted to "come clean" about it, somebody would have probably wanted to silence her. There could be plenty of charges connected to a black market baby ring.

"I had nothing to do with any of this," Ty insisted. "And I don't want to get caught up in it. Lamar's dead," he said once again, and his voice still dripped with emotion.

Hallie was yet to be convinced that emotion was the real deal, and she reminded herself that everything Ty was saying or doing could be one big lie. And she wondered if she was staring into the eyes of a killer. Because if Ty wasn't telling the truth about Lamar and Kelsey, then he could also be omitting that he was the mastermind behind Kelsey's death and the attacks.

"I don't want to end up dead like Lamar," Ty went on, "so I'm not gonna talk to you two anymore. That's my right—not to talk to you. It's my right to get a lawyer, and that's what I'll do if you don't leave me alone."

Nick stared at Ty a long time, and like her, he was probably trying to suss out what was true or how much more to push. "You might want to go ahead and get that lawyer," Nick warned him. "Because if you've withheld one bit of information, I'll make sure you're charged with obstruction of justice and even accessory after the fact to murder. Think about that, Ty. Think hard. Because accessory to murder can put you behind bars for the rest of your life."

With that threat, Nick stood, pushing back the chair so that it made a shrill scraping sound over the gray linoleum floor. It caused Ty to jolt. Or maybe it was Nick's scowl and hard lawman's glare that made him react that way.

"He's scum," Nick muttered when Hallie and he went out of the room and into the hall. "He was in the militia and almost certainly knew that Kelsey had sold her baby to them."

"Yes," Hallie quietly agreed. "And if he knew about Kelsey selling the baby, then he was aware there was a black market baby ring."

It sickened her to think of David being handed over to people who only cared about how much money they could earn from selling him. Ty might have been the one to set this whole situation in motion.

And he might be David's father.

The DNA results weren't in on that yet, but the testing was in progress.

Hallie steadied herself a little with the reminder that there was no way Ty would get custody of David. She would see to it.

Nick touched the back of his hand to hers. "You okay?"

She nodded, not trusting her voice.

"Are you okay?" he repeated. Obviously, he could see that she was shaken.

Hallie considered plenty of things she could say to Nick. She trusted him enough to tell him her fears. Even her need to run with David if it came down to that. But she settled for a simple, "Thank you for everything you've done for me. I appreciate it more than I can ever tell you."

His eyebrow lifted. "Uh, that sounds a little like goodbye."

"It's not," she assured him, and because she thought they could both use it, Hallie brushed her mouth over his. "It's not," she repeated. "I just wanted you to know that I'm glad you're on my side."

A corner of his mouth lifted. "Always." Nick returned a quick kiss before they headed to Leigh's office.

Hallie felt the heat from the kiss. Was still feeling it when they reached the bullpen. But it came to a quick end. Because she spotted the man sitting in the reception area.

Darius Lawler.

Nick stepped in front of her even though Hallie figured Darius had been checked for weapons. Added to that, Leigh was right behind them, and there were three deputies in the bullpen. Each of them was armed and had their attention trained on the man. Darius would be stupid to attack them there, but people did stupid things all the time, and Hallie wasn't forgetting that Darius was on their short list of suspects.

"Why are you here?" Nick demanded.

"I, uh, sort of followed you." Swallowing hard, Darius stood. He yanked off the black San Antonio Spurs cap that he was wearing and clutched it in front of him. Hallie noticed his hands were shaking. "I parked off one of the side roads between your brother's ranch and town because I figured eventually you'd leave and I'd get a chance to talk to you."

Hallie hadn't seen a vehicle, but there were plenty of trails along that road that were practically smothered with thick trees. Darius could have hidden on one of those for hours, or days, without anyone noticing him. Of course, that begged the question—why had he done that? If the man had wanted to see them, why hadn't he simply called and asked for a meeting?

"How'd you know we were at the Triple R?" Nick asked, taking the question right out of her mouth.

"I heard about the shooting on the news," Darius answered. There was a tremble in his voice, too. "I figured that happened because of Hallie and you. Because someone was after you there."

Well, he hit the nail on the head with that one, but that didn't mean he hadn't been involved in the shooting.

"Were you at the Triple R last night?" Hallie came out and asked.

"No." Darius first seemed offended. Then, his expression moved to troubled. There was also trouble in his eyes when his gaze met hers. "But I have to talk to Nick and you. Not here. In private."

They wanted to talk to Darius as well, but Hallie had no intention of leaving with the man.

"You can talk in one of the interview rooms," Leigh suggested. "Not the one you just used but the one across from it," she added to Nick and Hallie. "Then, I'll want to speak to Darius, too. I recognize him from the militia raid files I've been reading, and I have some questions."

It made sense that Leigh would go over those since it was almost certain that what had gone on during the raid was connected to the attack at the Triple R. That particular attack had happened on her turf. At her home. And it could have resulted in the man she loved being hurt or even killed. This was no doubt as personal now for Leigh as it was for them.

"Why do you want to talk to me?" Darius asked Leigh.

"It's routine," Leigh answered without hesitation, and then she motioned for them to follow her, taking them to another hall, away from the room where they'd left Ty just minutes earlier.

Part of Hallie wanted to see how Darius and Ty would react to each other. And maybe they'd do that after they'd finished with Darius. Since Ty had confessed to being a militia member, it was entirely possible that the two knew each other. And maybe their relationship was much more than merely being members of the same militia.

Maybe they were working together on the attacks.

Hallie could practically feel the nerves coming off Darius as they went into the interview room, but he stayed quiet. The silence continued until Leigh had left them and closed the door behind her.

"I know who sent Lamar to kill both of you," Darius blurted out. "And you have to stop him from killing me, too."

Chapter Eleven

I know who sent Lamar to kill both of you.

Nick was very much interested in what Darius had just said, and he was betting the man would continue to point a finger at Steve. However, Nick was also plenty skeptical about the man's claim. Or anything else he had to say. After all, Darius had a criminal record, and even though he'd been an informant for the ATF, he'd also disappeared after the raid. Now, he was back and apparently willing to tell them who'd killed Lamar.

Well, maybe he was willing.

It was just as possible that Darius wanted some kind of deal. Maybe immunity from prosecution for any part he might have played in the black market baby ring or the other crimes that'd gone on at the militia compound. Depending on what that part might have been, Nick might be able to get him a deal in exchange for information that could be proven and verified. However, there'd be no breaks or deals if Darius had had a part in Kelsey's and Lamar's deaths or the attacks on Hallie and David.

"We're listening," Nick assured the man.

Darius swallowed hard, and his gaze darted around before it finally settled on Nick. "I don't want to die. I need some kind of assurance that you won't let Lamar's killer get to me. I want that in writing," he added.

So, a deal after all. Except it wasn't what Nick had been expecting. Darius hadn't mentioned immunity. Not yet anyway.

"What kind of assurance do you think we can give you?" Nick asked.

Darius didn't even pause. "A safe house. Maybe some ready cash, too. Nothing big. Just enough to tide me over until I can start fresh."

Nick studied the man's expression and body language, and he knew that Hallie was doing the same thing. Both of them were trying to figure out if Darius was on the up-and-up or if this was some kind of ploy. In Darius's mind, he might believe that his willingness to help them would make him appear innocent.

It didn't.

Nick had every intention of keeping him on the suspect list, and Hallie would feel the same way.

"And what exactly do we get from you if we provide a safe house and some cash?" Nick asked. "Do we get the name of the person who sent Lamar to kill us?"

Now, Darius hesitated but only for a heartbeat. "Yes. And I have proof."

The sound Hallie made was a soft groan of skepticism. Nick was right there with her, but Darius didn't seem the least bit bothered by their reaction.

"Proof," Darius repeated, looking Nick straight in the eyes. "But you'll have to give me a break on that, too."

"Will I?" Nick asked, continuing the suspicion.

Darius nodded and swallowed hard again. "Because I had to bend the law to get the info. I had to hack into someone's computer."

Nick leveled his eyes at Darius. "Hacking isn't bending the law. It's a crime."

"I know." Darius turned from them, and groaning, he paced across the interview room. "But I had to find out for sure. I had a gut feeling, and it turned out that my gut was right."

Nick didn't want to push the criminal part of what Darius had done. He could do that later. But for now, he simply wanted to know if the man truly had anything that would lead them to who was responsible for the attack. If he did, then Nick would have to try to figure out a way they could possibly use it. One thing was for certain, hacked info wouldn't normally be allowed into the chain of evidence, but if they had a name, Nick could look for other evidence to make an arrest.

"What'd you find?" Nick demanded.

"This." Darius stopped pacing long enough to pull some folded papers from the back pocket of his jeans. "I printed it out so you could see for yourself."

Nick took the papers, and while Hallie went to his

side, he unfolded them. It was three printed pages from a bank account. But not just any account.

It was Steve's.

"You can see what's there," Darius went on. "Look at the deposits."

Nick was indeed looking, and he soon spotted what Darius must have considered "proof." There were electronic deposits of three thousand dollars. Six of them. And those had all been made in the two months prior to the militia raid. There were also other deposits in smaller amounts. Some withdrawals, too, but none of them were large enough to indicate criminal activity.

"It's payment for the babies just like I said," Darius insisted. "Greer Boggs, the militia leader who died in the raid on the compound,, transferred that money to Steve for the babies. That was Steve's cut."

Nick had to admit that it was interesting, maybe even suspicious, but it didn't prove that Steve had done anything wrong. "How do you know the payments came from Greer?"

"Because I heard that's what Greer paid for kids. Three grand to the person who actually brought the babies to the compound. The birth mom or dad got more, of course. Sometimes, thousands more."

Since Greer was dead, he wouldn't be able to dispute or confirm that, but Nick suspected the birth parents had indeed received compensation for the ones who'd been sold. Of course, other children had simply been stolen. They'd learned that after the raid and once the babies had been identified. Someone would have had to do the kidnappings. Maybe Steve. But it could have just as well been Darius or for that matter, any other member of the militia. Including Ty.

Nick stared at Darius. "You heard all of that about payments for babies," he stated, his voice all lawman. "Just how much did you know about the black market operation?"

"Just bits and pieces. I swear that's all." Darius groaned and used his forearm to wipe away the sweat on his face. "I didn't put it all together until later when I got to thinking back about things I'd heard." He paused. "And one thing I heard was that there was an ATF agent on the take. Then, the night of the raid, somebody tried to kill me. The person shot at me, and I'm pretty sure it was Steve."

That got Nick's full attention. It was plenty bad enough to accuse an agent of profiting off stolen or sold children, but now Darius was tacking on a claim of attempted murder.

"You didn't actually see Steve take the shot at you?" Hallie pressed.

"No, but I know it was him." Darius pointed to the paper that Nick was still holding. "Look at the second page."

Nick did, and he felt the immediate tightening in his stomach at what he saw there. No deposits here. But there was one large withdrawal for six thousand, and the money had been taken out just four days ago. Right before this whole ordeal had started with Kelsey's death.

"Steve used that money to pay off Lamar," Darius insisted. "No way would Lamar have gone after the two of you like that if Steve hadn't paid him to do it."

Nick wasn't so sure, but he couldn't dismiss it, either. Lamar had stayed under the radar when it came to the militia, so maybe the money had been incentive to get him to go to the Triple R.

But why?

If this all came back to David, and Nick believed that it did, then why had Lamar risked his life to get the child? It'd been a crazy long shot to come onto the ranch when there was that much security. Yet, Lamar had been there. Nick needed to dig deeper, but for now, he had to finish dealing with Darius.

"I'll arrange for you to stay at a safe house for a couple of days," Nick told the man. "Then, depending on what else we learn, we can make more permanent plans." He took out his phone and made the call to get that started. What he didn't do was spell out to Darius that the *permanent plans* might include a jail cell for him.

"Thank you," Darius blurted out when Nick had finished the call. "You saved my life."

Hell, maybe he had. If Steve was dirty, then he might indeed try to tie up all loose ends. Including Darius.

"Just wait here," Nick instructed. "I'll talk to Sheriff Mercer and see if one of her deputies can do guard duty until Agent Mark Wilder from the ATF shows up here to move you to the safe house."

"You trust this Agent Wilder?" Darius immediately asked.

"I do." That was the truth.

Nick had made the request personally rather than simply putting in the paperwork and having it processed. This way, fewer people would know where Darius would be taken. Steve no longer had access to official ATF information channels, but that didn't mean he still didn't have contacts.

"Wait here," Nick repeated to Darius, and Hallie and he left to go talk to Leigh. However, his phone rang before they even reached her office.

"It's Miriam," he said to Hallie, and while they were still in the hall, he took the call on speaker.

"Veronica just contacted me," Miriam said without any sort of greeting. "She wants to see Hallie again."

"Did she remember something?" Hallie quickly asked.

"I'm not sure, but she insisted that you come, that it was important she speak to you right away."

Hallie looked at him, and Nick nodded. "We're in Dark River," he told Miriam, "but we'll head to the hospital right now." He ended the call as they made their way back to the bullpen.

"I hope Rosa doesn't mind spending more time with David," Hallie murmured, taking out her phone no doubt to call the woman.

"I'm sure she won't," Nick said, and he got assurance of that when he heard Rosa tell Hallie that it wouldn't be a problem, that she'd be with the baby as long as they needed her to be.

"You're leaving?" Leigh asked when she spotted them from the doorway of her office.

"Yeah, we need to go to the hospital in Lubbock to speak to David's foster mother," Nick answered. "Any chance Vance or one of your other deputies can follow us there?"

Leigh nodded and gave Vance a signal that it was time to head out. While the deputy was walking toward them, Nick filled Leigh in on what was happening with Darius.

"You really think Darius is right about Steve?" Leigh asked when Nick had finished.

"Heck if I know, but I'll check into it once we're back from Lubbock." He slipped the bank account pages into his pocket, and Hallie and he headed out with the deputy.

The reminder of the danger was always with Nick. However, it was even stronger once they were outside. He didn't see anyone who appeared to be a threat, but he remembered Darius saying that he'd hidden on one of the side roads. Nick had to stay vigilant to make sure that didn't happen again. Because the next time, it could be someone ready to attack them.

"There's no way we can use those hacked bank records to get a warrant to see the rest of Steve's financials," Hallie commented. "But we might be able to use them to get him to confess."

Yeah, that would be a best-case scenario. And it was also an unlikely one since it would be a confession that could land him in jail. If Steve was actually guilty, he might just decide to try to kill them on the spot. Still, Nick had every intention of confronting the former ATF agent about what Darius had given them.

"We might also be able to trace the account number on the deposits," Nick added. "That wouldn't be admissible either since Darius obtained it through illegal means, but if the money leads back to Greer or someone else in the militia, we could maybe do a sort of reverse money trail."

She made a sound of agreement. "It'd be easier to convince a judge to issue a warrant for accounts connected to the militia than it would be to let us poke into Steve's."

And that's what Nick was counting on. There was no love lost between him and the Brothers of Freedom, and anything linked to them could be considered tainted. Of course, it was highly likely that any such accounts had already been closed, but even if they had been, there might be old documents the tech people could dig up.

They'd only gotten a few miles out of Dark River when Nick's phone rang again, and he got a jolt of worry when he saw that it was Leigh calling. Hell. He hoped nothing had gone wrong with Darius. Or at the ranch. He used the hands-free phone to answer, and seconds later, Leigh's voice poured through the SUV.

"David's fine," Leigh said right off the bat, because

she obviously knew they'd be alarmed about the possibility of something going wrong at the Triple R. "I'm calling about a report that I just got from the crime lab. The bullet taken from Lamar's body didn't match any of the weapons that Cullen or the ranch hands had on them. The lab also ran the gun that Lamar had with him when he was killed. No shots had been fired from it."

Nick opened his mouth to say something but closed it. Then, he cursed. They'd known there was a second man on the ranch, but this meant the guy had been the one who'd fired those bullets in the direction of the hands.

"There's more," Leigh continued. "And I'm guessing you won't consider this good news either. Lamar's tox screen showed he had the same barbiturate cocktail in his system that Veronica did."

Well, hell. There was only one conclusion he could come to about that. "Lamar was set up," Nick grumbled.

"Looks that way," Leigh concurred. "Well, unless he decided to get higher than a kite before he trespassed on a secured ranch to commit a felony or two. And not only that, he also somehow chose to use the same combo of drugs that Veronica's kidnapper had."

Nick was certain it hadn't gone down that way. More likely, Lamar had been a loose end that the second gunman, or his boss, had wanted to snip off. Maybe because Lamar had had some kind of info that would ID the actual person who had put this dangerous plan in motion.

And that led Nick right back to Steve, Ty or Darius.

Ty and Darius were at the Dark River Police Department. For now anyway. That meant two of their suspects couldn't get to Hallie and him. Heaven knew where Steve was, but Nick kept looking around to make sure they weren't being followed by either Steve or a henchman their attacker might have hired.

Nick ended the call with Leigh so he could better keep watch. And so he could glance at Hallie to see how she was doing. Not well, apparently. She was probably hoping that the crime lab would be able to give them something that would lead to the ID of the second man. But it was a dead end.

Since all three of their suspects were linked to both Lamar and the militia, they would almost certainly all have connections to the second man as well.

"We'll keep digging," Nick assured her. It was the best he could offer right now, but the best would eventually lead to finishing this.

When they reached the Lubbock hospital, Nick parked but waited until Vance had pulled in next to him before Hallie and he got out. They hurried inside with Vance right behind them.

"We shouldn't be long," Nick told the deputy. Vance nodded and took a seat in the waiting room.

Nick and Hallie didn't waste any time making their way to Veronica's room. As expected, there was a guard outside her door and they had to show ID before being allowed inside.

"Thank you for coming." Veronica's voice gushed

out, a mixture of both worry and relief. "I remembered some things that I need to tell you."

It was exactly what Nick had wanted to hear. Now maybe what she recalled would actually help them.

"I didn't want to talk about it over the phone," Veronica continued. "God, I'm so sorry, Hallie, for thinking you'd done this to me."

"It's okay." Hallie went closer, sitting on the edge of the bed and taking the woman's hand to give it a gentle squeeze. "What did you remember?"

"His mask. It was a man." Veronica's breathing was way too fast, so Nick hoped that Hallie could keep her calm enough to get through this. "He's like a blur, but I saw him. Well, I saw the mask anyway."

"Can you describe anything about him?" Hallie asked, and yeah, she kept her tone soft and soothing. "Height? Weight?"

"Average, I guess. Nothing stood out about him. He wasn't overly muscled," she added. "You know, not a bodybuilder."

Darius, Ty and Steve all had lanky builds even though Steve was a good fifteen years older than Ty. Darius had scruff while the others were clean-shaven, but a mask would have covered any facial hair.

"Okay, that's good," Hallie assured the woman. "What about his voice? Do you recall anything he said to you?"

"Yes." Now, Veronica's mouth trembled. "He said

a lot of things to me." She paused and squeezed her eyes shut.

"Did he have an accent?" Hallie asked when Veronica didn't continue.

She shook her head. "He sounded Texan to me. He kept his voice muffled, but I'm pretty sure he sort of drawled."

Again, that didn't eliminate any of their suspects since they were all Texans. "He threatened you?" Nick asked, deciding that's what was causing the fresh round of stress on Veronica's face.

"He did. Not at first." Veronica opened her eyes and stared at him. One look verified the stress was there, too, in her gaze. "While I was drugged and dizzy, he showed me Hallie's picture and said she was the one responsible, that she was the one who'd done this to me. He said it over and over again."

A form of brainwashing by implanting some false memories. It obviously hadn't worked though because it hadn't gotten Hallie tossed in jail.

But maybe that hadn't been the point?

It was possible the kidnapper just wanted to muddy the waters of the investigation, and the quickest way to do it was to implicate Hallie. That, in turn, put pressure on Nick to defend her, and it had spurred Child Protective Services to step in and try to take the baby.

"What else did the man say?" Nick continued. He took a few steps closer and sat in the chair next to the bed so that he'd be eye level with Veronica.

"I might have imagined it," she started. Then, she stopped and shook her head. "But I don't think so." Veronica reached for the cup of water on the bedstand and gulped some down. "I believe he said he was *the badge*. Not that he had one, but that he was one. That people trusted him." Her voice broke. "And that he could get to me any time he wanted."

Well, hell. Nick mentally replayed each word, and he could see this from two angles. If Steve was her attacker, he might have told her that to keep her from saying anything she might suddenly remember. But Darius or Ty could have used the ploy to frighten Veronica and try to set up Steve. More of those planted false memories to muddy the waters.

So, they were back to square one.

"He can't get to you any time he wants," Nick assured the woman. "You're being protected, and you'll continue to be even after you're out of the hospital." He paused, studied her worried expression. "If you'd like, you can stay with Hallie, David and me after you're released."

Though if she'd heard about the latest attack, she might want to steer clear of the Triple R. That was especially true since the woman obviously wasn't the primary target. Hallie and David were. That meant Veronica could be in more danger simply by being around them.

The woman's eyes immediately filled with tears, and while Nick wasn't always good at interpreting that sort of thing, he thought these tears were from relief and gratitude.

"Thank you," Veronica murmured. "That's so kind. But I don't want David to see me with all these cuts and bruises. It might scare him. I think it'd be best if I went to my sister's place in San Antonio. Her husband's in the military and they live on the base. There's a gate with guards."

Nick nodded. That kind of security would definitely make it harder for Veronica's kidnapper to get to her again. "I'll talk to Detective Gable about providing you transport and an escort to get to San Antonio," he told the woman, confident Miriam would agree to this idea.

Veronica muttered another thank-you and turned to Hallie. "Do you really think the man who hurt me is the badge?"

Hallie took her time answering. "I don't know. But Nick and I are trying to find out. In the meantime, we're going to keep David safe."

Veronica managed a small smile and then leaned over and brushed a kiss on Hallie's cheek. "I'll come and see all of you once everything is settled. Thank you for taking care of Hallie and David," she added to Nick.

Though it was good to hear, Nick didn't need her thanks for doing that. He was invested in making sure no one harmed them. Of course, he was invested in Hallie because he was falling for her. Heck, maybe he'd fallen months ago, but what he was feeling for her was growing fast and strong.

His feelings for David were growing, too, and he figured a lot of people would be shocked about that. Unlike many of his friends, he just hadn't felt the need to have a baby in his life.

But that was changing.

One thing was for certain—he'd need to figure out how to keep Hallie and David in his life long after the threat had ended. He couldn't just let them walk away.

Hallie gave Veronica a hug. "Call me when your doctor says you can be released."

"I will," Veronica assured her.

The moment Hallie and he stepped outside, his own phone rang. "It's Leigh," he told her.

He wondered if she'd found something else in the report from the lab. However, at the sound of Leigh's voice, Nick knew it was much more than that.

It was bad.

"Get back to the ranch now," Leigh blurted out. "The hands spotted another gunman."

Chapter Twelve

Everything around Hallie felt still, as if the air were holding its breath. But there was nothing still or on hold inside her. She was silently screaming. And praying. Lots and lots of praying. She was also wishing that she could just teleport herself to the ranch so she could be with her baby.

After they'd run out of the hospital and climbed into Nick's SUV as fast as was humanly possible, he'd put on his portable flashing lights, and behind them, Vance had both the cruiser's lights and sirens going. Now that they were out of Lubbock, they were going well past the speed limit, and still it didn't feel nearly fast enough.

There was a gunman on the ranch.

And David was in danger.

That reminder only revved up her fear even more, and Hallie tried to shut down the worst-case scenarios that were firing through her head. She couldn't go there because it would make her lose it, and she needed to keep herself together in case she had to fight once they got to the ranch.

A sound shot through the SUV, causing Hallie to gasp before she realized it was only Nick's phone that she had gripped in her hand. He'd given it to her at the start of his frantic drive so he could focus on the road. Even though her hands were shaking, Hallie answered the call on the first ring.

"I'm at the ranch," Leigh immediately said. "There's been no gunfire, and the hands have gone out to search for the intruder who tripped a motion detector. I'm heading out as well, but until you get here, I'm having Cullen stay inside with Rosa, Dawn and David."

"You stay with them, too," Hallie begged. "Whoever got onto the ranch is after David. He'll try to get in the house and take him, and he won't care who he hurts or kills in the process. I want him caught, but more than that, I want David safe."

Leigh's brief silence probably meant she was giving that some thought. "All right. I'll stay until I can get another deputy in place. How far out are you?"

"Ten minutes," Nick answered. Despite the high speed, he was also keeping watch around them. A reminder for Hallie that all of this could be a ploy to try to kill them on the road.

Or when they drove onto the ranch.

"Any idea which direction the gunman was going?" Hallie asked Leigh.

"None. Cullen thinks once he triggered the sensor by the back fence that he dropped down, out of the line of sight of the cameras. The detectors apparently won't pick up ground movement because if they did, small animals would always be setting them off." Leigh paused. "Obviously, that's a weak spot that Cullen will have fixed first chance he gets."

Yes, a definite weak spot, but it also wouldn't be fast or easy for a person to belly crawl from the back fence all the way to the house. Hallie didn't know how many acres that was, but the Triple R was one of the largest ranches in the county. A crawl like that would take hours.

"I'm going inside the house now," Leigh continued a couple of seconds later. "When you get here, check in with me before you just drive onto the grounds. I don't want any of you caught in the cross fire."

Hallie didn't want that, either, but she remembered Nick saying that the SUV was bullet resistant. The cruiser would be, too. That didn't mean the gunman couldn't manage to get off a kill shot, but it wouldn't be as easy as shooting into the house.

"Cullen and Dawn will make sure David is down on the floor and away from the windows," Hallie muttered when Leigh ended the call. She mentally repeated that assurance, trying to hold on to hope that her baby would be okay. If she didn't, the panic would start eating its way through her.

"They will," Nick assured her. "They'll protect David with their lives."

Hallie hung on to that, too, and since she couldn't do anything else, she just continued to pray and keep watch around them. Each wooded area they passed had her holding her breath. Because there could be a second gunman, one willing to pin them down with gunfire so they couldn't make it to David in time.

She recalled that Darius had hidden on one of the side trails, so Hallie made a point of looking at those, too. She didn't see anyone or anything suspicious, but she doubted their attacker would just wait for them out in the open.

They were still several miles out from the ranch when Nick's phone rang again. Like before, it was Leigh, and the woman spoke the moment Hallie answered.

"The gunman has jammed the cameras on the motion detectors," Leigh blurted out.

Sweet heaven. That brought on the panic, and Hallie had to fight it. It wouldn't help David if she lost it.

"We have no way of knowing where the gunman is, so watch the road when you come in," Leigh added.

Hallie wished the gunman would be close to the road because that meant he wouldn't be near David. Of course, that thought took her back to the possibility of there being two of them. If so, they could split up and do both. She already had her gun out, but her grip tightened on it.

"What about the security system?" Nick wanted to know. "Did he manage to jam it, too?"

"No. It's working," Leigh assured him. "For now anyway. Obviously, though, he might try to disable it if and when he gets closer to the house. All the doors and windows are locked," she added.

"You're still with David?" Hallie asked.

"I am," Leigh replied. "We've moved Rosa and him into the shower stall of one of the other guest bathrooms on the second floor. It has a stone interior and is away from any windows. I've positioned Dawn right outside the shower, and Cullen and I are guarding the door."

That meant David had three armed people protecting him, but if the gunman broke in, he might be able to shoot Cullen and Leigh. Or he could draw one of them away by creating a distraction elsewhere in the house.

"We're nearly there," Nick muttered, and Hallie figured that reminder was for her, to help her hang on.

"Cullen says to park on the east side of the house," Leigh informed him. "You can park right by the side doors, and that way you won't be out in the open too long."

Of course, a split second might be too long, but it was a chance Hallie would have to take. She had to get to her son.

"Call me if you spot anyone. I'll do the same," Leigh instructed, and she ended the call.

With the tires screeching on the asphalt, Nick took the turn toward the ranch. With each passing second, Hallie's heart pounded even harder. The nerves fired like lightning beneath her skin.

"Wait until I've disarmed the security alarm," Nick warned her when he braked to a quick stop by the east side door.

His hands were steady as he took out his phone to

do just that, and the moment he plugged in the codes, they threw open the SUV doors.

And they were instantly stopped by gunfire.

The shots came at them, a barrage of bullets that had them diving back into the SUV. The bullets slammed into the front of the vehicle, the sound of metal ripping into metal.

"Reset the security system," Hallie blurted out. "A second gunman could get into the house."

Obviously, Nick had already considered that because he was punching in the codes so that anyone who did try to get in would trigger the alarms. That way, Leigh and Cullen would have a heads-up that trouble was heading their way.

After he'd finished with the security system, Nick tossed his phone onto the seat and glanced around. Hallie did the same, both of them looking for the gunman. She didn't see anyone, but the shots were all coming from the back of the house. Maybe from the pasture beyond that if the shooter was using a rifle.

A bullet slammed into the windshield of the SUV. It didn't come all the way through, but the glass cracked and webbed, making it impossible to see out of it. The gunman fired another shot into the same spot.

Then, another.

Until finally the window gave way, and the pellets of safety glass spewed right at them. Nick grabbed her arm, pulling her down onto the seat.

The pain shot through her. Not because she'd been

hit but because her wounded arm bashed against the seat. She could have sworn she saw stars, but Hallie had no intention of letting the pain stop her from trying to pinpoint the gunman. The shooter might use this as a chance to try to move closer so he could kill them.

She heard the sound behind them, and Hallie turned to see Vance getting out of the cruiser. The deputy kept cover behind his door, but he started firing, sending his shots in the direction of the gunman.

"Stay down," Nick told her. "I'm going out the back of the SUV so I can use the cruiser for cover and return fire."

Hallie didn't like that plan at all, but she didn't get a chance to try to talk him out of it. Or stop him. Nick scrambled over the seats and lifted the hatch back door. She lost sight of him for a couple of heart-stopping seconds, but then she saw him take up position next to Vance. Both of them fired at the gunman.

The sound of the repeated blasts was deafening, and she prayed that none of the shots were getting into the house. Thank God David was on the second floor and in the shower stall, but that didn't mean he couldn't be hurt by flying glass. It also didn't mean a shot couldn't go through the wall and ricochet into him.

Choking back the possibility of that, Hallie forced herself to listen, and she glanced back at Nick and Vance. They'd quit firing, and both peered over the door toward the back of the house.

Where it was eerily silent.

Hallie counted off the seconds in her head. Still silent. The gunman had stopped shooting, and that meant if none of the ranch hands could stop him, he was probably getting away.

"Stay in the SUV," Nick warned her. "He might be waiting for one of us to come out."

True, and then he could gun them down. But waiting wasn't easy. Not when Hallie desperately wanted to make sure David, and Nick, were okay.

Nick's phone rang again, the sound of it jolting through the silence, and she answered it when she saw Leigh's name on the screen.

"David—" Hallie managed to say.

"He's okay," Leigh assured her. "We're all okay. What about the three of you?"

Hallie looked back at the men. "I don't think they're hurt. We're holding our positions."

"Do that," Leigh agreed. "I'm going to the back windows to see if I can spot anyone. Cullen is on the phone now with one of the hands to find out what they saw."

Good. Well, it was good if the gunman hadn't managed to get into the house, but she doubted that Leigh, Cullen or Dawn would just drop their guard. She certainly wouldn't, but as a minute crawled by, then another, Hallie's chest muscles eased up enough so she could take a full breath.

"I don't see anyone from the window," Leigh finally told her. "Not a gunman, not any of the hands."

From over the phone, Hallie heard Cullen calling

out something to Leigh, and she prayed it wasn't bad news. "Cullen said the hands all took cover once the shooting started," Leigh stated. "They'll head out now to start looking for him."

No way could the gunman have already gotten off the ranch, but it was possible he was hiding.

Waiting.

Maybe to make his escape or maybe to launch another attack. Once they were inside, Hallie would make sure that Cullen would order a search of every inch of every possible hiding place.

After several more minutes had passed, Nick and Vance finally stepped out from the cruiser. Nick came toward her, opening the SUV door. He looked rock steady. No surprise there. But she suspected this had shaken him as much as it had her. She got proof of that when he pulled her into his arms and brushed a quick, much-needed kiss on her mouth.

"We need to look through the house," Nick explained. His voice was steady, too. He positioned himself between her and the back of the house, and he took his phone from her. "Vance and I will do that once you're with David. Keep your gun ready," he added.

She nodded and waited while Nick started pressing the code to disarm the security system. However, before he could do that, someone called out to them.

"Don't shoot," the person yelled, and it was a voice that Hallie immediately recognized.

Steve.

NICK TOOK AIM at Steve when the man peered around the front of the house. Hallie and Vance followed suit, whipping up their guns at the same time and pointing them at the former agent.

"Don't shoot," Steve repeated. He leaned out, lifting his hands in the air.

"Give me a reason why I shouldn't," Nick snarled.

"Because I'm not the one who fired those shots at you," Steve insisted.

Nick wasn't convinced of that one bit, but it did seem stupid for Steve to hang around after an attack. Then again, maybe he decided there wasn't a way for him to escape so he was going to use the ploy of being innocent.

"Cover me while I frisk him," Nick muttered to Hallie and Vance. "If he makes a wrong move, shoot him." He added that last part in a voice plenty loud enough for Steve to hear.

"I didn't fire those shots," Steve repeated.

With his hands still up, Steve stepped out from the house and started walking toward them. Slow, easy steps. Just like the ones Nick was making to get to him. Behind him, he figured Hallie and Vance were doing the same. Hopefully, they were also keeping watch around them. Because if this was a ploy, a second gunman might try to finish this.

Nick kept his attention pinned to Steve. "Then, what the hell are you doing here?" Nick demanded.

"I came out to talk to you about the messages you've been leaving. You said you needed to see me."

"I do," Nick replied, "but it's a strange coincidence that you'd show up at my brother's ranch during a gunfight."

"Trust me, if I'd known there'd be a shoot-out, I wouldn't have come. I know this looks bad, but I didn't have anything to do with what happened. Somebody's trying to set me up."

Maybe. But Nick wasn't taking any chances. The moment he reached Steve, he took hold of the man's shoulder, pushing him against the side of the house. Steve assumed the search position with his palms flat on the wall and his legs apart. Nick took the gun that he found in Steve's slide holster, and he handed it back to Vance.

"I want that bagged and sent to the lab," Nick instructed. "I want to know if it's been fired recently."

"It hasn't been," Steve insisted as the deputy took it.

That was possibly true. A smart move would have been to ditch the weapon used in the attack, and that's why Nick would ask Leigh to have her people do a thorough search of the area. If Steve had truly tossed a gun, they needed to find it. The good news was that it couldn't be far, since the attack had just taken place.

"We have to go in and talk," Steve said, glancing over his shoulder.

Nick scowled. "That's not going to happen."

Steve huffed. "But it's not safe out here."

True enough, and that's when Nick glanced at Hallie. "Why don't you go ahead in and check on David?"

Nick added that last part to entice her to go inside. He knew she was desperate to make sure the baby was all right, and he hoped that would outweigh her need to stay with him while he kept an eye on Steve. The man didn't look as if he was ready to attack, but looks could be deceiving. Pretending to be innocent could all be part of his plan to get close enough to kill them.

"Steve and I will move this conversation to the cruiser," Nick added when Hallie didn't budge. "And Vance will be with me."

Even with that extra security measure and her urgency to see David, Hallie still hesitated, but then she finally nodded. "I want to know everything he says," she insisted, tipping her head to Steve.

"Will do," Nick promised her.

He motioned for her to stay put a moment longer while he texted Cullen, asking his brother to come downstairs and "escort" Hallie through the house. No way did Nick want her walking in on the gunman if the SOB had somehow managed to get inside during that short period of time when the security system had been turned off.

It took a couple of minutes, but Cullen finally opened the side door. His brother glanced at him, then at Steve. "You need help?"

"Just with Hallie." And Nick left it that, but Cullen understood that he didn't want her alone.

Cullen nodded and put his hand on the small of Hallie's back to get her moving. Nick waited for them to go inside where he was sure Cullen would reset the security system before Nick ushered Steve to the back seat of the cruiser. Vance got behind the wheel, but he turned so he could keep his gun trained on Steve.

"Start talking," Nick demanded, "and if you don't convince me you're innocent, I'll arrest you here and now."

"I'm innocent," Steve spat out. The man had obviously gotten back some of his temper, but it was only a quick burst of heat. Nick watched that heat come and go, and then Steve gave a weary sigh. "Someone's been making deposits into one of my bank accounts."

"Do tell." Nick made sure there was plenty of sarcasm in that.

Steve stared at him, and he seemed to be confused that Nick would know about the money. "I found out yesterday, but I didn't want to say anything because, well, because I thought it'd make me look guilty."

"Do tell," Nick repeated.

The anger flared in Steve's eyes again. "Yes, *do tell*," he snarled. "Someone's setting me up, making deposits and then a withdrawal. I must have been hacked or else someone got hold of the account numbers and managed to do some finagling."

"And you didn't notice until yesterday?" Nick challenged.

No angry reaction this time, but Steve looked as if he wanted to kick himself. "It's not my main account. It's one my folks set up for me when I was in college. I have a credit card connected to it, and I use it every now and then when I buy something online from a site I haven't done business with before. There are also some small deposits that go into it from some investments that I made years ago."

"And you didn't notice the other deposits and withdrawal until yesterday?" Nick pressed.

"I rarely check it, okay?" That answer flew out with some more anger. "But I got a call. An anonymous tip," he snapped like profanity. "The caller said you were digging into my accounts so I had a look. And it was there. The deposits, the withdrawal. They were there, and someone's setting me up."

Nick held back on any sarcasm and studied the man's expression. Temper, yes. It was firing in his narrowed eyes. But temper would be a reasonable reaction if what Steve was saying was true.

"I want Deputy Pickering here to take you to the Dark River PD so he can test your hands and clothes for gunshot residue," Nick stated. "And like I already said, your gun will be tested, too. Then, I want you to turn over all your financials to a forensic accountant at the crime lab. After that, you can give Deputy Pickering your statement as to why you were at the ranch today. Spell out everything. *Everything*," Nick said with emphasis.

Nick waited, figuring Steve was going to protest doing at least one part of his demands. But he didn't.

The man simply nodded.

Of course, his agreement didn't mean he wasn't the gunman. Like insisting he was innocent, he could be co-operating to make himself look as if he'd had no part in any of this. Steve could have already covered his tracks with the financials along with using gloves during the gunfight. It was also possible that he'd faked an anonymous call by using a burner cell to contact himself. Still, when Steve did that whole *spelling out everything*, he might give them something they could use to hang him.

"Go ahead and take him to Dark River," Nick told the deputy. "I'll let the sheriff know what's going on."

Vance nodded, and as Nick had done with Hallie, the deputy waited until Nick had temporarily disarmed the security system and had gone inside. Nick immediately glanced around but didn't see anyone. Nothing was out of place, and there were no signs that any of the bullets had gotten into the interior. That was a small blessing considering all the shots that'd been fired so close to the house.

He made his way up the stairs, following the sound of the voices to one of the guest rooms—of which the house had many. Cullen or Leigh had chosen a room in the center, probably so that they'd be able to keep an eye on the stairs while also keeping the baby away from the back of the house where the shooter would have most likely been approaching.

As expected, Cullen was still in the doorway with Leigh right by his side. The whispered conversation they were having came to a quick halt though when Nick approached.

"Is everyone okay?" he asked.

"Fine," Leigh answered. "Vance just texted me to say he was taking Steve Fain to the police station."

Nick nodded. "Steve says he's not the shooter, that he'd just come here to talk to Hallie and me."

"You believe him?" Leigh asked.

Nick shrugged. "If he's guilty, then he's playing a mean game of reverse psychology." Then again, the stakes for him were high, so desperation to cover his tracks could be driving him.

From the bathroom, he could hear David babbling and Hallie's laughter. Mercy, it was good to hear that, and he wanted to see them for himself. But for now, Nick needed to finish up with Leigh and his brother.

"All right, what's wrong?" Nick demanded. And his mind started to come up with some bad possibilities. Like maybe one of the ranch hands had been shot. Or worse.

Leigh dragged in a deep breath. "Right before I had to leave my office because of the attack, I called the lab to check on the status of David's DNA sample that the Lubbock PD took. I explained I was the primary investigator on a murder that might be connected." She paused. "It's missing."

It took Nick a couple of seconds to figure out what she meant. "The DNA is missing?"

Leigh nodded. "It was logged in, but both it and the original sample are gone. The record of it has been wiped from the system."

Nick could only groan. "That sounds like an inside job," he remarked. Because a glitch wouldn't have removed it like that.

"It probably was. One of the crime lab techs, Chaz Billings, was reported missing this morning. About an hour ago, Lubbock PD sent someone to his apartment, and they found him dead. *Murdered.*" She emphasized the word. "It appears he'd been dead for a while, hours at least. They're estimating he was killed shortly after Miriam made the request for David's DNA to be checked for a match in the databases."

Hell. That meant they couldn't rule out Ty since he wasn't taken into custody for the bar incident until that evening.

"There's more," Leigh went on, lifting her phone screen. "There happened to be a working security camera on a shop just up the street from Chaz's apartment. This is a shot of the man who paid Chaz a visit shortly before he was murdered."

Nick studied the photo. It was grainy, but he could still see the visitor's face. And there was no mistaking exactly who it was.

Darius.

Chapter Thirteen

Hallie eased David into his crib for the night. She'd considered just holding him. To make sure he stayed safe. And to make sure her own nerves stayed steady. Holding him had a way of forcing her to stay calm. But she also needed to talk to Nick, and even though David wouldn't know they were discussing things like attempted murder, it was best if he stayed tucked in his bed.

She brushed a light kiss on the baby's cheek and backed away from him. Watching him for a few more seconds before she took the monitor, and leaving the sitting room door slightly ajar, she went back into the main part of the guest room to find Nick. She didn't have to look far. He was pacing while he had his phone pressed to his ear. It was exactly how Hallie had left him when she'd taken David into the makeshift nursery–sitting room to feed him a bottle and get him down for the night.

Nick looked more frustrated though than he had just a half hour earlier. Something Hallie hadn't thought possible. But it'd been a day of frustrations what with the attack, the bank allegations against Steve, the missing DNA and then the surveillance photo of Darius going into a dead man's apartment.

Hallie wouldn't have minded the frustration if they were closer to putting the attacker behind bars, but there were still too many unknowns. Maybe Nick was getting some of the answers they needed.

Rather than just jump right into the questions she wanted to ask, Hallie went to him and pulled him into her arms. She didn't kiss him. Didn't make this the heated contact that it usually was when they touched. She simply held him. And it worked. She could feel some of that frustration drain from him. That helped some of the tension drain from her own body as well.

He pressed his mouth to the top of her head, lingering there for a moment, before he kissed her cheek. It was still chaste. Well, almost. Since this was Nick, it was impossible to take out all the heat. That was probably why he eased back from her. It wasn't the time for them to test the limits of their willpower against this fierce attraction they had to each other.

"There's a mix of good and bad news," he said after dragging in a long breath. "Which do you want first?"

Hallie sighed. "The bad." Best to get the worst out of the way and then end things on a high note. Well, as high as possible, considering their circumstances.

He nodded, and even though he'd moved out of her arms, Nick still kept hold of one of her hands. "Darius isn't at the safe house, and they don't know where he is."

Her sigh turned to a groan. "He just walked out?"

"Pretty much. He told the agent he was going on the back porch to get some fresh air, and he left. Darius didn't have a phone with him. He'd had to surrender it before he went to the safe house so it couldn't be tracked."

Hallie thought about that a couple of moments. "So, Darius doesn't know you want to talk to him about Chaz Billings and the missing DNA?"

"That's more of the bad news. Chaz's murder leaked to the press. Not just the story of his death but also the surveillance picture of Darius. So, it's possible Darius saw the reports on TV or read about it on the internet."

That was more than possible since safe houses almost always had televisions and even modified laptops. The laptops had plenty of safeguards on them, but it wouldn't have kept Darius from getting basic news.

"If I were giving him the benefit of the doubt, I'd say he saw them, panicked and ran because he thought somebody might kill him. But I'm not giving him the benefit of the doubt," Hallie added. "He could have run because he killed Chaz and knew the cops would soon arrive to arrest him."

"Yeah," Nick agreed. "It could have gone down that way. Or Steve or Ty could have been the one who killed Chaz. The camera shows Darius going in and leaving through the front door, but Miriam said someone had tampered with the lock on the back patio door, too. There's not a camera in sight anywhere back there."

So, why wouldn't a killer have used the door where he wouldn't be detected? Maybe Darius hadn't known about the camera. And if he had, perhaps he'd decided to use it to play to his advantage. Go in through the front door, leave Chaz alive and then return through the back to kill him. If there was enough of a time lag in between the first and second trips to Chaz's place, then Darius might believe the official time of death would clear him.

And it might.

"No word from the medical examiner on time of death?" she asked.

Nick shook his head. "Miriam put a priority on that so we should have it soon. And that brings me to some good news. Well, a mixed bag of good news anyway. Miriam sent David's DNA to two different places. The crime lab where Chaz worked and another one, Merricor, that's contracted with Lubbock PD. Merricor will be able to run the sample tomorrow."

Hallie agreed that it was indeed a mixed bag of news. They needed to know if there was a match in the databases because it could possibly help them ID their suspect. But it would also ID David's father, and Hallie knew that could create plenty of trouble for her.

Because his biological father could try to claim him.

Nick must have known exactly what she was thinking because he pulled her back to him. Kissed her. Then, he looked down at her. "Change of subject. Not an especially happy change, but it's something you need to

know. Steve gave Vance and Leigh his total coopera-
tion. Leigh didn't have any evidence she could use to
hold him so he left, but we should know the results of
his gun and the gunshot residue test very soon."

Steve would have been an idiot not to cooperate,
especially after he'd shouted his innocence and tried
to explain away why he'd been at the ranch. So, that
meant neither of those tests might tell them anything
they could use for an arrest.

"The forensic accounting will take a little longer,"
Nick continued. "Maybe weeks. Apparently, it's hard
to speed up that sort of thing."

Hallie didn't doubt that, but she was hoping Leigh
or Miriam had managed to put in the lab request as a
priority. That could maybe cause things to move a little faster.

"And what about Ty?" she asked.

"He posted bail for the drunk and disorderly and
left." Nick paused. "And, yes, I know that means all
three of our suspects are free to come after us again.
That's why I want to move David and you to a safe
house."

Nick stared down at her, obviously waiting for her
reaction, but it took Hallie some time just to process
what he was saying. Since they'd arrived at the ranch,
she hadn't considered moving elsewhere.

But she should have.

In hindsight, she should have accepted that their attacker knew their location and would continue to come

at them. Maybe next time, he'd succeed in actually getting into the house. The fact that he'd been able to jam the cameras on the motion detectors meant that he might be able to jam the security system as well.

"When do we leave?" she asked.

The corner of his mouth lifted in a smile that held no humor. "Late tonight or in the early hours of the morning. I've started the wheels turning, but I need to make sure everything is in place."

Hallie didn't question exactly what he was putting in place. This was Nick, so the plan would be thorough with David's safety his top concern. Of course, nothing was fool proof, but if they could conceal their location from their attacker, it would buy them not only some safety but some time as well. Time they could use to continue the investigation and finally put an end to the danger.

She leaned in to kiss him again, and this time, she decided it wouldn't be chaste. It would be long, hot and needy. Especially needy since she was feeling a lot of that at the moment. But his phone rang before she could put her mouth on his.

"The call is being routed through ATF dispatch," he said when he looked at the screen. He hit answer and put the call on speaker. "This is Agent Brodie."

"Nick," the caller said, sounding relieved.

It was Darius.

"Where the heck are you?" Nick demanded.

"Someplace the killer won't find me. I couldn't stay

at the safe house." Darius talked fast, his words running together. "Not after I heard Chaz got killed because I figured if the killer could get to Chaz, he could get to me."

Hallie listened for anything that would clue her in that Darius was lying. Then again, he'd seen a picture of himself on a surveillance camera so he'd had some time to concoct a story that sounded believable.

"Start explaining," Nick insisted. "You knew Chaz?"

"Yeah," Darius answered. "We weren't like best buds or anything, but I knew him. We were sort of friends."

"Really?" Nick sounded as if he wasn't buying that. "How did a criminal informant and a lab tech become *sort of friends*?"

"I met him at a club a couple of years ago, and we hung out every now and then."

Again, his answer was fast, and the emotion was high in his voice. Like a man who was scared. Or a man who wanted them to think he was scared.

"Why were you at his place yesterday?" Nick continued.

"'Cause he called me and asked me to come over, that's why. He knew I'd belonged to the Brothers of Freedom and that I'm a CI, and he wanted me to know that somebody had threatened him. The person left a note on his car, ordering him to destroy some DNA on the baby who'd been found in the raid."

"David's DNA?" Nick questioned.

"Yeah, that's right. Chaz was scared. I mean, really

scared 'cause whoever left that note said they'd kill him if he didn't get rid of the DNA."

Nick huffed. "And even though Chaz often does work for the cops, he didn't call Lubbock PD about a threat like that? Instead, he called you, a criminal informant who was sort of a friend."

Hallie figured Darius had no trouble picking up on the skepticism in Nick's voice. That's probably why the man huffed.

"He thought I'd have contacts, and he didn't know which cops he could trust," Darius said with another fast answer. "It was the same for the ATF. He didn't know if it was safe to call them. I decided the same thing after I heard he was killed. I wasn't gonna trust them. Not you either, Nick."

"Well, you're going to have to trust somebody because you're a person of interest in Chaz's death," Nick informed him. "You'll need to go into Lubbock PD and give a statement."

"No can do," Darius insisted. "I'd probably get killed just walking in that place. I'm just gonna lay low for a while, and once you've caught Chaz's killer, then I'll come in and give all the statements you want."

Nick opened his mouth, no doubt gearing up to tell Darius why he couldn't wait to do that, but before he could get another word out, Darius ended the call. Cursing, Nick worked his way back through dispatch, getting them to try the number, but Darius didn't answer.

"Darius was probably using a burner," Nick muttered. "Still, I'll ask dispatch to try and trace the call. I'm also sending a text to Miriam," he added, already typing the message.

Hallie read the text and saw that Nick asked Miriam to check Chaz's phone to see if he'd made a call to Darius. If Chaz had, that would support what Darius had just told them. But Miriam didn't come back with a quick response. Since it was well after normal duty hours, it was possible that the detective was taking a much-needed break.

Something that Nick needed. Heck, she needed it, too.

"You barely touched your dinner," she said, remembering that he'd left most of the cheeseburger and fries on his plate. "Why don't you head down to the kitchen and get us both a snack?"

Hallie had purposely added "both" so that Nick would indeed get some food—which he would then hopefully eat. He took a step toward the door, but then he immediately turned back around to face her.

"Are you actually hungry?" he asked.

No. In fact, she hadn't managed much of her own dinner, but she nodded, still hoping this would lead to him eating.

He didn't budge though.

Nick continued to stare at her, and on some muttered profanity, he reached out and slid his hand around the back of her neck. He drew her to him. Not a hard pull but a gentle, barely there touch.

It was more than enough to get her against him.

The slow pace also gave her a chance to back away. Which she didn't do. They landed body to body. And very soon, mouth to mouth. The kiss was surprisingly gentle, too. That was somewhat of a miracle considering how fast he could build up the heat inside her.

Even though he kept things slow, he still managed to take those kisses to her neck. Deep. Intimate. Stoking fires there, too. But then he stopped and looked down at the monitor she still held.

"You'll hear David if he wakes up?" he asked.

"Yes," she assured him. Hallie set the monitor on the nightstand and brought Nick right back to her.

The next kiss had an edge to it. Not so gentle, and the urgency was already there, building. Building. Building. Until Hallie knew this particular make-out session wasn't going to stop with just kisses and touches. It would lead them straight to bed.

And she was so ready for that.

It had nothing to do with needing a break. Or wanting a distraction. No, this was all about Nick. About both wanting and needing *him*.

Hallie showed that need by kissing his neck, and she was rewarded with his groan of pleasure. It also kicked things up a notch. He ran his hand over her breast, cupping her and swiping his thumb over her erect nipple, which was pressing against the cup of her bra.

Soon, the touching wasn't enough, and he slid his hand up her top, shoving down her bra, so his clever fingers were on her. So was his mouth. He deepened the kiss and sent the flames inside her soaring.

The ache spread. Grew. Until the kisses and the touches only made her need him more. Nick must have thought so, too, because he stripped her shirt and bra off and went after her breasts with his mouth.

The pleasure speared through her, and Hallie had no choice but to grip him and ride out the wave. He circled her nipple with his tongue before he drew it into his mouth.

She heard the sound of need that came from her throat. Felt it continue to build until she could take no more. With her hands trembling she managed to get his shirt off and then went after his zipper. But Nick put his hand over hers to stop her.

"I don't have a condom," he said, but he winced, no doubt remembering that she couldn't get pregnant because of the injuries she'd gotten in the militia raid. "But I was recently tested during my annual checkup, and I'm okay."

"I haven't been with anyone…in a very long time," she said. "And I'm okay, too."

Because she didn't want him to change his mind about this or have too much time to think, she pulled him to her. Obviously, Nick had no intention of backing off. While he doled out more of those scalding kisses, he shimmied her out of her jeans and panties. In the same motion, he dropped her on the bed—with him on top of her.

He was lean but still with plenty of hard muscles. Perfect. Just as she'd known he would be. His weight felt good on her and added to the heat. Of course, so did the kisses and touching.

And the man could touch.

Nick slid his hand down the center of her body. Touching her until she wanted to beg for release.

Hallie did something about getting that release. She went after his jeans. No easy feat since she had to also remove his boots, but it felt like a huge victory when she got him down to his boxers. Then, she got him naked.

Yes, he was perfect.

She pulled him back up her body so they'd be face-to-face, but he dropped another kiss on her stomach. On her scar, she realized. He'd know just how much that injury had cost her, and that's why it made the kiss even more special.

"Last chance to change your mind," he muttered, giving her the out that she in no way wanted.

Hallie took hold of him, lifting her hips to meet him as he pushed inside her. The pleasure fired through her, robbing her of her breath. She couldn't speak, either, but she could certainly feel, and Nick made sure she felt a lot with those long hard strokes inside her.

The pace was almost frantic, fueled by the need and what they felt for each other. This wasn't just sex, and Hallie knew she'd have to deal with the consequences of that. Later. For now, she just let Nick take her on the wave. They rode it together, hard and fast. Until Hallie felt the climax ripple through her.

Nick watched her, as if trying to hang on to the moment for as long as he could, but with his mouth covering hers, he soon followed.

Chapter Fourteen

Nick gave himself some time to just hold Hallie. Time to come back down to earth, too. Then, he rolled her to the side so that he wasn't crushing her. He didn't let go of her though. He needed her in his arms, so that's where he kept her.

Later, he might have regrets about taking her this way, but he didn't think so. In fact, he thought the only regret he might have would be that he hadn't done this sooner. He'd always wanted Hallie. Always cared for her. Too bad it'd taken the danger from the attacks to bring them together.

"Don't overthink this," Hallie whispered, brushing a sleepy, sated kiss on his neck.

He frowned, not sure what she meant by that, and he hoped like the devil that she wasn't about to tell him that this could be nothing other than sex. Because it meant a lot. It meant everything. He eased back from her just a little so he could look down at her to tell her that, but his phone rang.

Cursing the interruption and the fact that he didn't

actually know where his phone was, he scrambled out of bed and finally located it in the pile of clothes on the floor. When he saw the caller, he cursed again because it was Miriam, which meant this could be important.

"What?" Nick answered, well aware that it wasn't exactly a friendly greeting, but he would have liked at least a couple more minutes with a naked Hallie.

"Your mood sounds about as good as mine," Miriam grumbled, "and it's probably not going to improve much with what I have to tell you."

Nick cursed, scrubbed his hand over his face but also checked the monitor to make sure David was still asleep. He was. "What happened?" Nick asked.

"Chaz's phone wasn't at his apartment, his work or in his car," Miriam explained. "My guess is his killer took it."

Nick figured she was right about why Chaz's phone was missing. Of course, if Darius was the killer, then it might have helped clear him if they could confirm that Chaz had indeed called him.

"I can get phone records," Miriam went on, "but it'll take time. Oh, and speaking of time. We got a TOD, and Chaz was killed at least two hours after Darius left his place."

That didn't mean Darius hadn't been the one to murder him though. "Someone tampered with Chaz's back door," Nick reminded her. "Could have been Darius."

"True. Or any number of suspects. But I'll worry about that tomorrow. I haven't slept in over twenty-four hours and am about to hit the sack. Don't call or text me unless it's really important," Miriam added right before she ended the call.

"I heard," Hallie said when he looked back at her. She got up and started gathering her clothes. Except she didn't just pick them up, she started putting them on. "Maybe the phone records will tell us something."

Nick was banking on that because he was tired of all these leads not going anywhere. And now he was frustrated because he needed to make a call about those phone records. Yes, Miriam had said she would do it, but it might move faster going through the ATF.

"I should call about the safe house, too," he muttered, pressing in the number and putting the call on speaker.

While Nick waited for an answer, he hooked his arm around Hallie's still bare waist and caught her for a kiss. A long, deep one that he had to cut short because Agent Beverly Watkins answered. She was someone he trusted with his life, so Nick had asked her to make the arrangements for the place for Hallie and David.

"I was just about to message you to let you know that the safe house is ready," Beverly immediately said. "I'm sending the first part of the address from one number, and I'll send the rest from another phone."

That was a security precaution that Nick very much appreciated so it'd be harder for someone to hack the info. Seconds later, the texts appeared, and he saw that the safe house was in Lubbock. That was good since it'd put them close to the ATF office and Lubbock PD.

"I've got two agents already in place," Beverly went on, "and it's stocked with the supplies you said you'd need. I'm texting you the security code for the place now. Just type it into the keypad by the door. When will you be heading there?"

Nick looked at Hallie and got her nod. "Soon. I'll just need to arrange for Dark River PD to provide some backup during the drive."

"All right, I'll let the agents know to expect you. Stay safe, Nick," the woman added.

Nick thanked her and ended the call just as his phone dinged with another text. The security code this time.

"What about a vehicle?" Hallie asked, pulling on the rest of her clothes. The peep show was over. "Your SUV has bullet holes in it."

He nodded. "Cullen has an SUV that's bullet resistant, and he moved David's car seat into it. It's in the garage so we don't have to go outside."

Hallie nodded, and while he knew she appreciated the bullet resistant part, it would still be a dangerous trip. Unfortunately, staying put wasn't a safe bet, either.

He doubted that Leigh had turned in for the night, but Nick texted her, asking how soon she could have backup for them. She answered right away.

Twenty minutes, her message read. Two deputies will be outside the garage when you're ready. They'll be in a car, not a cruiser.

Yeah, the cruiser would have been like a huge red flag. This way it would maybe look as if two vehicles were leaving the ranch at the same time. It might draw suspicion but not as much as a police car would.

"I'll get the diaper bag packed," Hallie murmured, heading into the makeshift nursery.

She'd been gone only a couple of seconds when his phone rang, and he saw Miriam's name again. "I thought you were getting some sleep," Nick said. When Hallie hurried back in, he put the call on speaker and mouthed, *It's Miriam.*

"That was the plan," she grumbled. "But the plan changed. Apparently, there's a fire to be put out. An actual one," she said, clarifying her statement.

"Where?" Nick snapped, hurrying to the window to look out. He didn't see anything, but he wouldn't put it past their attacker to set a fire to try to smoke them out.

"At Merricor Labs," Miriam answered.

It took him a moment to connect the dots. "That's where you sent the second sample of David's DNA."

"Bingo. I'm heading over there now to get a look at it, but word is the place is going up in flames."

Nick cursed.

"Yeah, my sentiments exactly," Miriam said. "Obviously, our guy is getting desperate. Watch your back, Nick. I've got a bad feeling this SOB isn't going to wait much longer to come after you again."

HALLIE KNEW IN her gut that Miriam was right. The person after them had already come at them twice here at the ranch, and since it was now dark, it would be the perfect time to try again. It twisted her into knots to think he might succeed. That he might actually get to David, but she also knew that Nick and she would do whatever it took to stop that.

She forced herself to focus her attention not on the gnawing fear but on putting David's things in the diaper bag. In the main part of the guest room, she could hear Nick going through the closet to pack a bag for her. There'd no doubt be clothes, formula and such at the safe house, but since they had to wait for the deputies to arrive, they might as well bring some of the things with them.

David was still sound asleep so Hallie kissed him, and carrying the monitor with her, she went back in the room with Nick. One look at him, and she knew this was eating away at him, too.

"Miriam texted me," he said. "The fire at the lab was set on a timer."

Hallie couldn't stop herself from groaning. A timer meant the killer might not have been near the lab for hours. He could be anywhere. Including already near the ranch.

Setting the small suitcase aside, Nick went to Hallie and pulled her into his arms. "It'll be okay. It has to be okay."

Yes, because she couldn't consider the possibility of losing him or David. She loved them. Except it was more than that.

She was in love with Nick.

Maybe she always had been. Always would be. But now wasn't the time to distract him by telling him that. Especially since it was something that he might not want to hear.

There was a light tap at the door that had both Nick and Hallie reaching for their guns, but they backed off when they heard Leigh say, "It's Cullen and me."

Nick hurried to the door, opening it. "Is something wrong?" he immediately asked.

"No," Leigh assured him. "No motion detectors have been triggered, and the hands haven't spotted anyone."

Not yet. But Hallie knew that could change any minute.

"We wanted to run something past you," Cullen said, leaning against the jamb. "But I should tell you up front that it's something you're probably not going to like."

"All right," Nick said. "What is it?"

It was Leigh who continued. "We think it might be a good ploy for Hallie and you to leave as if you're actually heading for the safe house. But don't take David with you. Instead, let him stay here."

Cullen was right. Hallie didn't like it, and she quickly shook her head. "What if the killer comes here while we're gone?"

"You won't be far," Leigh explained. "The idea is to lure the snake out while you're with my two deputies. I considered taking Hallie's place, but she and I don't look anything alike. Ditto for any of my deputies. There's just not enough resemblance. If the killer is using binoculars or surveillance equipment, he'd realize that it wasn't Hallie."

Leigh was right, and with just a glimpse in the SUV, the killer would know it was a ploy. And he'd backtrack to the ranch.

"We can keep David's car seat in Cullen's SUV," Leigh went on, "so it appears that he's with you. That might stop the killer from firing shots directly into the vehicle."

"Might," Hallie repeated though she wasn't so sure.

It was true that the break-in at her house had almost certainly been a kidnapping attempt, but it'd been different at Nick's house. Any one of those shots could have hurt David. Just as anyone could hurt him tonight if the killer fired into the SUV when David was with them.

"The security at the ranch isn't perfect," Cullen went on, "but at the first sign of trouble, we can have Rosa take David into the bathroom with the stone shower like she did before. Leigh and I can stand guard to make sure no one gets in." Cullen looked Hallie directly in the eyes. "No one will get past us."

She believed him. Or rather she believed that he'd do everything humanly possible to protect David. But it might not be enough.

Nothing might be enough.

That thought crashed into her, twisting and turning her fears. Fears that wouldn't end until they got rid of the threat.

Hallie looked up to see what he thought of this plan, and he leaned in, kissed her. "I trust Cullen and Leigh."

So did she. And she also knew just how determined the killer was to get to them. If he came after Nick and her, maybe they could finally stop him.

Hallie nodded, not trusting her voice, and she went back into the nursery so she could kiss David on the cheek. She almost wished he would wake up so she could see him. But that would feel like a goodbye.

Like the last time she'd be with him.

She couldn't let herself think that way. Couldn't let that kind of doubt take hold in her mind.

"The deputies are here," Leigh told her when she came back into the guest room. Rosa was already there, too. "It's Cecile Taggart and Andy Mendoza. They're both good cops, and I've filled them in on the investigation. They've seen pictures of all of your suspects."

Nick muttered a thanks. "I was thinking about driving south for about two miles," he said. "Then turning on Miller's Point by the pond."

Hallie knew the spot. It was a wide road with few curves. She also didn't know of many ranch trails there. Of course, she doubted the killer would be hiding out there. No. He was likely watching the ranch and would follow them.

"Miller's Point goes back into town," Hallie pointed out.

Nick made a sound of agreement. "It does, but I don't want to lead this SOB into town. I'll make another right

turn before Dark River and then head back in this direction. It'll hopefully seem as if we're making sure we
don't have a tail."

Yes, it would, and it was possible they would indeed
have that tail. The killer could maybe follow them with
his headlights off. There was enough of a moon that it
might be doable. Then, he could just stay a safe distance behind them and watch where they were going.
Or maybe he'd just look for the best place to attack.

"I'll take good care of your little boy," Rosa told
Hallie, and she gave Hallie's hand a reassuring squeeze.

Nick didn't linger. Maybe because he thought Hallie
might change her mind. And she considered it. Considered a lot of things. But each possibility came back to
what was best for David. She prayed this would turn
out to be the right decision.

They went down the stairs, and after Hallie grabbed
a baby blanket, they threaded their way through the
house to get to the door that led into the garage. There
were several vehicles inside but only one was an SUV
so they headed there, and she saw that David's car seat
was indeed already in the back, facing the rear of the
vehicle. Since they wanted to make the killer believe
David was with them, Hallie climbed into the back,
rolled up the blanket so it mimicked the baby's shape
and put it in the car seat.

She also drew her gun, holding it on her lap so she'd
be ready.

Nick's eyes met hers in the rearview mirror as he

opened the garage door. He was no doubt trying to give her some reassurance, and Hallie tried to do the same for him. But she figured there was little chance of it working for either of them.

As Leigh had said, the car with the two deputies was right there, and when Nick backed out and drove away, it followed. Not close though. Still, it was near enough for Hallie to get a look inside when they drove past the front security lights of the house. Deputy Andy Mendoza was behind the wheel, and Deputy Cecile Taggart rode shotgun.

Nick didn't have to remind Hallie to keep watch. She looked for any lights or moonlight glinting off a vehicle. Or a gun. She didn't see anything, but she'd have to stay vigilant for however long this took.

It was entirely possible that the ploy would fail, that they would just end up driving around before giving up and returning to the ranch. Then, they could get David and start a new drive. One that was much riskier than their current situation. Still, they had to get David out of danger, and that meant either luring out the killer or taking him to the safe house.

Nick didn't speed even after he took the turn from the ranch to the main road. As usual, there were no other vehicles, and thankfully the moonlight illuminated the pastures and the trees. There were shadows, of course. Places for a killer to hide, but so far nothing.

It didn't take them long to reach Miller's Point, and when he turned onto the road, Hallie saw the long stretch of white fence on both sides. The pond, dark and sprawling, was on the right.

The deputies made the turn behind them and continued to stay back. However, they hadn't gone far before Hallie saw something.

The slash of headlights.

Not from behind or in front of them but on the left side of the SUV. Nick's side. He obviously saw it, too, because he looked in that direction. But it was already too late.

The huge semi seemed to come out of nowhere, and it crashed right into them.

NICK DIDN'T HAVE time to try to get the SUV out of the path of the collision. Nor was there time to even brace himself for the crash. He could only pray that Hallie and he would survive this.

The semi wasn't hauling a trailer, but it was still plenty big and heavy. It was like a blast from an explosive when it rammed into the SUV. And mercy, it hurt. Almost instantly, Nick could feel the pain as the impact caused his body to whiplash to the side.

His seat belt snapped tight, vising his shoulder and chest. In the same exact second, the side and front airbags deployed, both of them knocking into him and smothering him in a cloud of powder that had been packed around the bags. He was pinned to the seat, but at least the door had held.

Well, partly.

It was caved in, jutting against the side of his body. If it hadn't been for the airbag, the door would have crushed him. Obviously, their attacker had chosen to hit this side of the vehicle instead of the one with the infant car seat where David was supposed to be. The impact could take out Hallie and him while minimizing the risk to the baby, especially since the car seat was reinforced to keep a child as safe as possible during a collision.

From the back seat, he heard Hallie moan. She was in pain, and it caused him to scramble into motion. He prayed she wasn't hurt badly. Everything inside him yelled for him to get her to safety.

He couldn't see the semi, but Nick heard the driver rev the engine. Maybe backing up to come at them again. Or he could be going after the deputies in the other vehicle. Either way, Nick knew he didn't have much time.

"Hallie," he managed to say even though the powder was making him cough.

He fought for air. Fought to punch down the bags, too. Then, he had to get out of the seat belt, which wasn't easy since it was so tight that he could barely move. That's when he realized his arm and shoulder were throbbing like a bad tooth. Maybe something was broken, but he was hoping that it was just jammed from the collision.

"Hallie," he repeated, leaning over the seat to get to her.

She groaned and was clearly dazed. There was also blood on her forehead. Her window was cracked, but the safety glass was still in place so maybe she'd hit her head on the car seat. Thank God, she was still conscious because Nick wasn't sure he'd be able to carry her out of there before they got hit again.

He heard the shouts of the deputies, telling the driver to stop, but Nick figured there was zero chance that would happen. Because this was the killer. And he was no doubt ready to ensure that, this time, he didn't fail.

The revving of the semi's engine got louder, and the deputies fired shots. Probably to try to hit the driver. Nick hoped they would be able to do that, but he couldn't risk just sitting there.

Cursing the pain in his shoulder, he stretched over the seat and managed to get his hand on the handle to open the front passenger's door. But touching it was as far as he got.

The semi plowed into them again.

This time it wasn't a high-impact crash like the first one. Going much slower, the killer drove the front end of the semi into the side of their SUV. And he started pushing. Slowly shoving the SUV through the fence.

Even over the gut-tightening sound of metal crunching and grinding into the SUV's door, he could hear the gunfire continue. Cecile Taggart and Andy Mendoza were obviously trying to stop this, but Nick was pretty sure not all the shots were coming from the deputies.

It sounded as if the killer was shooting, too.

Or maybe the killer had brought a henchman with him. And now they were going after Leigh's deputies. Nick hoped that Andy and Cecile would take cover. He certainly didn't want them getting too close to the semi where they could be crushed or be in the path of those shots being fired.

Tucking his gun in the back waistband of his jeans, Nick went for the door handle again, but he also looked out the window. To make sure Hallie and he weren't about to be attacked by someone coming from that direction.

They weren't.

But they were in trouble.

The semi shoved the SUV through the fence, crashing through the wood and sending it flying. Some of the pieces cracked the glass. But Nick saw where the killer was shoving them.

Straight into the pond.

He had no idea how deep the pond was, but no way would the killer want to jeopardize David so the SOB must have figured the baby wasn't actually with them or that he could get to David in time to save him. Not save Hallie and him though. No. The killer would want them dead.

"Hallie, we have to get out now," Nick snapped.

She was obviously still groggy and was mumbling something he didn't catch. He didn't want to risk dragging her over the seat for fear she had internal injuries, but he had to get her moving. Scrambling over the front seat, he got the door open just as the semi's engine revved again. The truck bashed them right into the pond.

The water rushed over him. Dark and cold. The pain didn't help, either, but he fought through it, trying not to sink while he opened the back door of the SUV. He didn't quite manage it though. His head went under, but Nick fought to get back to the surface. He doubted the killer would just drive the semi into the pond, but if he did, it was possible the SUV would get trapped beneath it.

Hallie would be trapped.

And she could drown.

The reminder had him fighting even harder to get to her door, but before he could take hold of the handle, it opened, and Hallie practically spilled out into the water with him.

Somehow, she'd managed to keep hold of her gun. No telling how long that would last though. They both went down, the water covering their faces and rushing into his mouth and nose. It was no doubt doing the same to Hallie, and he could feel the panic coming off her in waves when she fought to get back to the surface.

They came up together, both of them gulping in breaths, both of them fighting not to sink again. If they did, they could die, and since the killer or his henchmen weren't rushing in to save the baby, that told Nick that their attacker had known all along they didn't have David with them.

"We have to move," Nick managed to say.

Of course, that was easier said than done. They weren't that far from shore, but it was too big a risk to try to get out right behind the SUV. The killer was almost certainly waiting for them to do just that.

There was plenty of light because of the semi's headlights and the moon, so Nick could see that Hallie's head was still bleeding. She also still had a tight grip on her gun. That was a good thing because wet guns could still fire, and they might need to shoot to defend themselves or to help the deputies stop this killer.

"This way," he said, leading Hallie away from the SUV.

Nick tried not to make any noise because he didn't want the killer tracking them, and he hoped the deputies' continued shots were keeping the killer inside the cab of the semi. That would limit his aim.

Hopefully.

"Officer down," Cecile called out, causing Nick's stomach to clench.

Andy had been shot. And was maybe dead. He couldn't hear the rest of what Cecile said, but he thought she was calling in the incident.

The gunshots had stopped, which was both good and bad news. Good because it meant no bullets were being fired at the deputies and them. Bad because it probably meant the killer was getting out of the semi and was looking for a better way to gun down Hallie and him.

Nick led her away from the SUV but toward the edge of the pond that had a cluster of shade trees. Unfortunately, those trees were a good fifteen feet away from the water. Every inch of that would give the killer a better opportunity to shoot them. However, if they got behind cover, Hallie and he could wait it out until help arrived. If Leigh wasn't already on her way, she soon would be.

Hallie's breathing was ragged by the time they reached the pond's edge, and it didn't help that the air was heavy. Like a wet blanket mixed with the exhaust from the semi.

"When you get out, run for the trees," Nick told her. He positioned himself so that he'd be in between Hallie and the semi.

She looked at him, and he saw all the fear and sadness. The determination, too. Hallie might be hurt, but she wasn't giving up. Their ploy had worked. They'd drawn out the killer. Now, they needed to deal with him.

Hallie made a sound of pain when she pressed her hands against the bank to hoist herself up. She'd probably torn out her stitches because there was blood on her arm, too. Soon, very soon, she'd get the medical care she needed, but for now, they had to stay alive.

"Run," Nick reminded her, shoving her the rest of the way out of the water.

She struggled to get to her feet, but the moment she had her balance, Hallie ran. Nick was right behind her. But they'd only made it a few steps before the next shot rang out.

Chapter Fifteen

Hallie ran as if her life depended on it.

Because it did.

She couldn't ignore the bullets as they slammed into the ground around her, but she forced herself to focus on getting to the trees. There, Nick and she just might make it out of this alive.

Her lungs were burning, and the pain in her head and arm felt fresh and raw. Throbbing. She ached everywhere, and her wet clothes and shoes weighed her down, making each step a challenge.

Almost there, she thought looking at the trees. Almost there. And she repeated it like a mantra with each step.

There were more shots. Then, more of the searing pain. She wasn't able to choke back the sharp groan when she felt the bullet slice across the side of her right leg. Not a direct hit, at least she didn't think it was, but mercy, it was already hurting. Worse, she was getting dizzy from the injury she'd gotten when her head had hit the side of the baby's car seat. She probably had a concussion. But she couldn't let it stop her.

Because she had no choice, she dropped to the ground, crawling the last couple of feet and then diving behind the first tree she reached. She lay there for only a second. Just enough time to gather her breath. Then, she turned, levering herself up and bringing up her gun to give Nick some cover.

And her heart stopped.

It just stopped.

Because he hadn't been behind her as she'd thought. He was at least ten feet away and was flat on the ground.

"Nick!" she called out before she could stop herself.

That, of course, had the shooter sending more bullets her way. But Hallie didn't let that stop her. She called out to him again and saw that he was alive when he lifted his head. She couldn't tell how badly he'd been hurt, but her mind began to fill in all kinds of bad possibilities.

She couldn't lose him.

That gave her a fresh hit of adrenaline to numb the pain and sharpen her focus. Hallie leaned out from cover and took aim at the man who was by the front end of the SUV. The SUV was partially submerged, but it was still giving him enough cover from Cecile so he could try to kill Nick and her.

Hallie fired.

Her shot made a pinging sound as it skipped off the SUV, but it had the shooter ducking. Nick must have caught the movement because he got up and scrambled behind a large boulder by the pond's edge. She hated that he wasn't with her, but the position would give him the best angle for taking out the gunman.

"Backup is on the way," Cecile yelled. "Leigh's staying put but sending help."

Hallie was thankful to hear that. Thankful, too, that Leigh would be staying with David. But that meant backup would have to come from Dark River, and it might not arrive fast enough. It was also possible that whoever Leigh was sending wouldn't be able to get close enough to provide any real help. She certainly didn't want them walking right into gunfire.

Hallie leaned out again, and after picking through the spearing headlights of the semi, she spotted the shooter leaning out as well. She couldn't see his face because he was wearing a ski mask, but she fired another bullet at him.

Then another.

Like before, he ducked back. But not before Nick also got off a shot. He lifted his body off the ground just long enough to fire.

Hallie wanted to cheer when she heard the man howl in pain. Nick had managed to hit him and maybe, just maybe, it'd turn out to be a kill shot. She didn't care if he bled to death as long as it put an end to the danger, but she had to wonder who was behind that mask.

Was it Darius, Ty or Steve?

It was too bad that their builds were so similar or she might have been able to tell which it was. Then again, it didn't really matter. All of their motives went back to David and the black market baby ring. Now maybe those motives would be the end of him.

"Andy's alive," Cecile added a moment later. "But he's hurt. I've called for an ambulance."

Hallie figured the reason Cecile was no longer returning fire was because she was tending to the wounded deputy. Maybe even trying to stop him from losing too much blood. Besides, with the shooter in front of the SUV, Cecile would have had to come out in the open just to be able to see him. No way would she have had a clean enough shot.

Nick lifted his head again, looking in the direction of the shooter, and when the man didn't show himself, Nick started to get up. The shooter had to have been watching because lightning fast, he fired a shot.

"Stay down!" Hallie yelled to him.

She tried to give Nick some cover by sending a bullet in the gunman's direction. Obviously, he wasn't dead after all, maybe not even bleeding out, but he did duck back into cover because of her shot.

Fifteen rounds of ammunition, she reminded herself. That's what she'd started with loaded in her Glock. Nick, too. But Hallie had lost count of how many bullets they had left. Probably not enough if they ended up having to hold this gunman off much longer.

Cecile and Andy were no doubt well armed with not only backup weapons but also extra ammo. If things went from bad to worse, she'd have to call out for the deputy to move into position to give them assistance. It was too bad that Hallie couldn't use the phones for that, but unlike their weapons, the cells were useless after going into the water.

She watched as Nick shifted to the other side of the boulder, and he took aim again. Hallie did the same. She kept her attention nailed to the spot where she'd last seen the gunman.

And she waited.

The pain was still there, throbbing. So was the fear. Because she knew at any second the gunman could deliver a fatal shot.

Several seconds crawled by, and Hallie finally saw the shooter. He leaned out, his gun already pointed at Nick. But Nick's and hers were already on him.

The three of them fired at the same time.

The shots were heavy blasts, all the more loud because they'd come in unison. Hallie immediately looked at Nick. To make sure he was okay. He was.

But the shooter wasn't.

Thanks to the semi's headlights, she saw his body stiffen. Saw the blood spread across the front of his shirt. And he dropped to the ground in a crumpled heap.

Hallie started to run to Nick, but the sound behind her stopped her. She whirled around.

Already too late to stop the gun from bashing against the side of her head.

"STAY DOWN," NICK called out to Hallie.

He had to see if the SOB was actually dead, and he didn't want Hallie coming out of cover until he was certain of it.

Bracing his shooting wrist with his hand, Nick hurried out from the boulder and around the pond. His boots sank into the boggy ground and there was still plenty of pain from his wrenched shoulder, but he ran as fast as he could. And he kept his attention nailed to the downed shooter. He definitely didn't want the guy using his dying breath to get off one last shot.

"Are you okay?" Cecile called out. "Do you need help?"

"Just stay with Andy," he told her.

Nick had no idea just how bad the deputy's injuries were, but maybe the ambulance would get there soon. Not just for Andy but for Hallie. He remembered the blood on her head so at a minimum she'd need stitches, but she'd also need to be examined at the hospital.

He cursed the gunman for being able to hurt her like that. For nearly killing them. If the SUV had flipped over when they'd been pushed into the pond, they could have drowned.

The engine of the semi was still running, the sound chugging and rumbling. Nick tried to block it out while he trudged around the pond's edge to get to the gunman. The guy still hadn't moved, and his gun was nowhere in sight. It was possible it had gotten tucked underneath him when he fell. It was just as possible that the guy was holding on to it until Nick got closer.

Then, the gunman could again try to kill him.

Nick considered putting a bullet in his leg just to make sure this wasn't a ruse. But instead he settled for scooping up a rock about the size of a walnut. He hurled it at the guy, smacking him on the head.

The gunman didn't move a muscle.

That was Nick's green flag to move closer. He watched the guy's arms as he rolled him over. His gun was there. Coated in blood.

No pulse, Nick learned when he pressed his fingers to the man's neck. Definitely dead. The gunshot wound to the chest had seen to that. Maybe a shot from his Glock. Maybe from Hallie's. Either way, this idiot wouldn't be trying to kill anyone else.

Since the guy's mask was covered with blood and mud, Nick grabbed the edge of it and eased it back enough until he saw the man's face.

And his heart went to his knees.

Because it wasn't Ty or Darius. Or Steve.

Nick had no idea who he was, which meant he was almost certainly a hired gun. And that meant his boss was likely somewhere close by.

He fired glances all around him, his attention settling on the trees where he'd last seen Hallie. Nick didn't see her now, but he had told her to stay down. He prayed that's what she was doing.

"Hallie?" he called out.

No answer.

So he tried again while he ran as if her life depended on it. Because it probably did.

In the distance, Nick heard the police sirens, the wailing sound cutting through the night and blending with his own ragged breath and his hurried footsteps. The air was thick. Heavy. And the bad feeling in the pit of his stomach was starting to claw its way to this throat.

Hell.

Hallie could be dead. The person who'd hired that henchman could have already killed her. But Nick tried to force that nightmare aside.

"Get down!" someone shouted.

Hallie.

It was her voice all right, but it was strained and muffled. Nick dived to the side just as the shot tore past him.

"No," Hallie yelled. "I'm not going to let you kill him."

Nick heard rustling. There was a fight going on, and he knew that Hallie was in the middle of it. Fighting to stop the killer from shooting him. Fighting to save her own life, too.

He got up and started running again. But he'd barely made it a step when there was another gunshot blast. Everything stopped. His breathing. His heart. Maybe even time itself.

Mercy, had he lost her?

The sound that came from his throat was feral and fueled by a slam of adrenaline and fury. He tore across the grassy strip and straight into the trees. Ready to kill. But he pulled to a quick stop when he saw Hallie on her knees.

She was alive, but there was even more blood on the

side of her head. And she wasn't alone. There was a man wearing a mask kneeling behind her, and he had a gun. Not pointed at Hallie.

But at Nick.

"Figured you'd come looking for her," the man growled. It sounded as if he was purposely trying to disguise his voice. "Then, I could finish you both off."

That put some focus back in Hallie's eyes, and she drew back her elbow, ramming into the man's ribs. He snarled a string of curse words and grabbed her by the hair when she started to scramble away.

Nick rushed forward. Or rather that's what he started to do, but the man stopped him with a single shot. Not at Nick. But at Hallie. Nick lost years off his life, and for a few horrifying moments, he thought the SOB had managed to shoot Hallie.

He hadn't.

Because just as the man pulled the trigger, Hallie threw her weight back, bashing her head into his face. Nick didn't know where the bullet went, and he didn't waste any time trying to figure it out. He charged.

Tackling the guy was a risk. Anything was at this point, but Nick wanted to try to get that gun away from him. Nick landed with part of his body on Hallie and the other part on the gunman. No way could he risk firing a shot since he might hit Hallie, so he punched him.

This time when the man cursed, he didn't disguise his voice. Nick instantly knew who he was.

Darius.

The sound Hallie made was pure anger, and Nick knew what she was feeling. This was the piece of scum who'd tried to kill them. Who'd repeatedly put David in danger.

Hallie drew back her elbow to ram the man again, but before she could do that, Darius managed to maneuver his gun.

He put it to her throat.

For an instant anyway. Just enough time to get Nick to stop. Then, Darius turned the gun toward Nick.

And he fired.

HALLIE THREW HER weight against Darius a split second before the man pulled the trigger. The shot missed Nick just as the other one had done, but she had no idea how long she could hold Darius off. He seemed hell-bent on killing them.

Yelling to boost her own adrenaline, Hallie shoved Darius again and scrambled behind one of the trees. From the corner of her eye, she saw Nick do the same thing. Thank God, he was alive. Now, they needed to make sure they both stayed that way.

When Darius had sneaked up on her and clubbed her, he'd also knocked her gun out of her hand, and Hallie didn't have a clue where it was now. She thought Nick had still managed to hang on to his weapon. Darius must have thought that as well because he took cover behind the other tree.

"I think this is what we call a standoff," Darius said, the mock humor dripping from his voice.

He threw something onto the ground in front of them. The mask, she realized when she glanced out.

"Why are you doing this?" she snapped. There was no humor, mock or otherwise in her tone. It was sheer frustration and bitterness. This man had caused them all so much pain, and it wasn't even over.

Darius laughed. Again, there wasn't any humor in it. "Don't tell me you haven't already figured it out. David's my kid."

She pressed her lips together, holding back the sob that wanted to break free. Hallie didn't want this monster to know how much it sickened her that he had any connection to her precious little boy. It was only a DNA connection, she reminded herself. Darius had no claim on David.

And he never would.

"You put your own son in danger," Nick snapped. He was obviously having a hard time reining in his rage, too.

"I need to get him so there won't be a link between me and the black market baby operation. And I will get him," Darius insisted. "No link, and with the two of you dead, no proof."

Hearing that only spiked her rage—and her disgust for this worthless man. Hallie didn't need to ask Darius what he'd done because the pieces all fell into place. Well, most of them anyway. Darius had known about the babies being held on the militia compound and hadn't bothered to share that info with the ATF. Worse, he'd intended for his own flesh and blood to be sold.

"Did Kelsey let you give David to the militia?" Hallie asked.

"More or less. Since I was the one running the baby ring and needed some more *product* to sell, I sort of made her an offer. I'd let her live if she gave me the kid." Darius chuckled. But Hallie thought she heard him make another sound. One of pain.

Had he been hurt in the scuffle?

Mercy, she hoped he had. In fact, maybe he'd shot himself when he'd tried to kill Nick.

"And when Kelsey started making noise about getting the kid back, you murdered her to silence her," Nick said, obviously filling in more of the pieces. "You're the one who's been trying to cover up that David would be a match to your DNA."

Darius didn't comment on that. Didn't have to. It was what made sense. He was, after all, a hacker and had been the one to give them Steve's bank records.

"You set up Steve," she stated.

"Yeah," Darius said, his voice a hoarse growl now, "and he'll take the fall for this. For all of this."

Not if she could help it. Once Nick and she were safe, they could clear Steve's name and assure Veronica that she wouldn't be attacked again. But Kelsey, Lamar and Chaz were dead. Darius or one of his henchmen had murdered them. No way to make good on that except to make sure that Darius spent the rest of his life in a cage.

She heard the soft clicks and saw the glow from a phone screen. Darius was texting somebody. Probably another hired gun. So, that was his plan. To have another person swoop in and help him.

"Nick?" Cecile called out. "Hallie? Where are you?"

"If you answer her, I start shooting," Darius warned them. He grunted, paused, continued. "I might miss. Might hit her."

Hallie wished she could signal the deputy to get down, but she couldn't risk moving out from cover. Darius was behind the tree directly across from her, and he'd certainly see her. Nick might have a chance though. He was to Darius's right and might be out of his line of sight.

Might.

But Darius was desperate, and so far he'd been very lucky about not getting caught. She very much wanted to do something to end his lucky streak.

Hallie saw the lights swirling from the cruiser as it approached the pond. More deputies, no doubt, and Cecile would fill them in. Well, fill them in as much as possible since Cecile probably didn't know exactly where they were.

"Nick?" someone called out.

It was Deputy Dawn Farley, this time, and Hallie caught a glimpse of the woman making her way to their submerged SUV.

"If you want her to live, tell her to stay back," Darius instructed. "Do it," he added in a snarl when neither of them spoke. "And if you tell her it's me with you, then she dies, too."

"Up here," Nick shouted to Dawn. "But stay back."

"Good job," Darius said quietly, and Hallie didn't think it was her imagination that he sounded weaker. He was grunting, too, and cursing under his breath.

She fumbled around on the ground and located a rock. It was big enough to make some noise so that's what she did. She flung it behind Darius and hoped like the devil that he took the bait.

He did.

Darius fired in that direction. And he also moaned in pain. Nick must have picked up on it, too, because he sprang out from the tree, heading straight for Darius.

So did Hallie.

Nick made it to Darius just a couple of steps ahead of her, and Hallie saw Nick ram his body into the man. Both of them went flying backward, but she focused on Darius's gun. She had to get to it to stop him from firing again. However, she also wanted to make sure no one sneaked up on them and got in some easy shots.

Hallie fought back her own pain and scrambled to the ground. The men were already in a life and death fight with fists flying. But she spotted Darius's gun— right as he was trying to bring it up to aim it at Nick. She did something about that.

Cursing Darius and the nightmare that he'd put them

through, she stomped hard on his wrist and got the satisfaction of hearing the bone snap in his hand. Darius yelled in pain. And she stomped on him again.

Blindly swinging his broken hand around, Darius reached out for her, but Nick stopped him. He knocked the gun away, causing Darius to yell again. Then, Nick bashed his fist into the killer's jaw.

Nick got right in his face and spoke through clenched teeth. "Move and I kill you."

No one who heard the threat would have doubted that Nick would do exactly that. Including Darius. She could see it in his expression. The surrender.

Or something.

Blood was on Darius's teeth and lips when he smiled, and he looked down at his stomach. At the blood there.

"I shot myself," he said, like it was a joke. "Aiming for Nick and I shot myself. I'm a dead man," he grumbled.

"Yeah, and I hope you rot in hell," Nick snarled.

Nick still had a white-knuckle grip on the front of Darius's shirt, and Hallie could feel the rage coming off him. He wanted to kill Darius. He wanted to use his hands to squeeze the life right out of him. She couldn't blame him. But she didn't want Nick to have to live with that.

Hallie reached down and gently touched Nick's shoulder. "If he lives, he'll do it behind bars. Every day, every minute for the rest of his life behind bars."

Her words must have gotten through to him because

Nick pushed himself away from Darius and stood. He still had his gun, and he kept it trained on Darius.

"Cecile? Dawn?" Nick called out. "I've got Darius at gunpoint. He's the killer."

"Are any of you hurt?" Dawn asked, and Hallie could already see the woman heading toward them.

"Yeah," Nick answered. "But Hallie and I will live. This SOB might not."

Darius chuckled again. It was dry as dust and laced with venom. He showed his bloody teeth again and looked Hallie straight in the eyes.

"I knew Nick and you would try to trick me. You wanted to make me believe you had the kid with you. But you wouldn't have brought him out with you like that. Before the fight even started, I sent someone to get David," Darius said. "I might be dying, but you'll never have the kid. *Never.*"

Chapter Sixteen

Before the fight even started, I sent someone to get the kid.

Those words fired in his head like gunshots. Nick had no idea if Darius was telling the truth, but Hallie must have thought it was at least possible because she took off running.

Or rather limping.

That's when Nick saw that her leg was hurt. It didn't stop her. She ran toward the cruiser just as Dawn made it to Nick and Darius.

"If Darius moves, shoot him, and keep watch around you," Nick told the deputy, and he took off after Hallie.

"The ambulance is on the way," Dawn called out to him.

Nick didn't acknowledge that. He ran, trying to eat up the distance between Hallie and him. It wouldn't do any good for him to remind her that whoever Darius had sent could be right here instead of with David.

Ready to gun them down.

It wouldn't matter to Hallie. Nothing would at this

point. It was the same for Nick. They had to get to David and make sure he was okay.

"I need a phone," Nick told Cecile.

The deputy tossed him hers, and Nick saw the blood on her hands. Andy was on the ground beside their cruiser, and Cecile had obviously been trying to staunch the flow of blood from what appeared to be a gunshot wound to the shoulder. It didn't look life threatening, not like Darius's injury, but Andy would need medical attention, fast.

"We're taking Dawn's cruiser," Nick added to Cecile.

"Vance and some others are on the way," Cecile said to him.

Good. They could do clean up and secure the scene, along with making sure Darius didn't make a miraculous recovery and start causing more trouble. Nick hated the idea of leaving Dawn alone with Darius and Cecile alone with Andy, but it couldn't be helped. No way was he letting Hallie go to the ranch alone.

"I'm driving," Nick insisted, getting behind the wheel of the cruiser.

Hallie didn't argue. Maybe because her leg was hurting too much for her to attempt it, or it could be that the fear had clamped her throat shut. Nick knew all about bone-deep fear right now. It didn't matter whose child David was. Nick loved him, and he intended to stop and kill any goon Darius had sent after the boy.

Since the semi was blocking most of the road, Nick had a very tight space to turn the cruiser around, but the moment he'd done that, he hit the accelerator and tossed Cecile's phone to Hallie.

"Call Leigh," he insisted. "Her number will be in Cecile's contacts."

Hallie managed a nod. A shaky one. Actually, just about every part of her was shaking, and he hoped like the devil that she wasn't going into shock. The blood on her hands didn't help, either, and it took her several tries to scroll through the contacts and press Leigh's number.

Nick sent up a whole lot of thanks when Leigh answered on the first ring.

"It's me. Hallie," she said. Her voice was mostly breath, but she cleared her throat. "Darius is the one who's been after us, and he said he sent someone to the ranch to take David. Please tell me David is okay." The tears began to spill down her cheeks with that last plea.

"He's okay," Leigh said. "But someone did trip one of the motion detectors."

Hell. Darius hadn't lied after all.

"Is the guy close to the house?" Nick demanded.

"I'm not sure, but Cullen went downstairs to make sure no one tried to break in if the intruder managed to jam the security. Who'd Darius send?" she asked.

"Don't know, but we'll be at the ranch in just a couple of minutes. I'll send Hallie inside to be with David, and I'll go look for this SOB."

Hallie didn't disagree with that plan though he figured once she had seen for herself that David was okay, then she'd want to have a part in putting an end to what Darius had started.

"I'll let Cullen know what's going on," Leigh assured him. "Be careful, Nick."

He would be, and that started by firing glances around them when he took the turn to the ranch. Hallie did the same. Nick spotted a few armed ranch hands patrolling the road, and he hoped the henchman was wearing a ski mask and didn't try to blend in with the other hands.

Just ahead, the lights from the house were cutting through the night. Enough light for Nick to see the movement to the right of the cruiser. Not a ranch hand but rather a man dressed all in black. And yeah, he was wearing a mask. Obviously, he hadn't thought about the ploy of blending.

Nick slammed on the brakes, threw the cruiser into park and opened the door. The moment he was out, he took aim over the top of the vehicle.

"I'm Agent Nick Brodie," he called out. "Put down your gun."

The idiot didn't, of course. He raised it.

Nick fired first.

His bullet slammed into the guy's chest. Probably a kill shot, but Nick hoped not. He wanted some answers first. Once he had them, he didn't give a rat if the guy lived or died.

"Call Leigh back and tell her what happened," Nick instructed Hallie.

That would hopefully keep her in the bullet resistant cruiser and not out in the open. Nick went in the open though. Keeping his gun ready, Nick approached the man who was now on the ground. He was bleeding all right, and unlike Andy, this wound did indeed look fatal.

"If you want me to get you an ambulance, you'll start talking," Nick snarled.

Of course, Leigh would almost certainly call for an ambulance, but the gunman didn't know that.

Nick kicked the guy's gun away and yanked off his mask. He didn't know him, but mercy, he was young. Probably not even old enough to legally drink. That didn't make Nick dole out any sympathy. Not when he'd done Darius's bidding and had come here to try to take David.

"Talk," Nick demanded. "Who are you?"

Groaning and clutching his chest, it took him a couple of seconds to answer. "Gavin Cross."

The name rang a dim bell in Nick's memory. "You were part of the Brothers of Freedom," he spat out.

Gavin nodded. Groaned.

Two of the ranch hands came running up, and both of them aimed their guns at Gavin. "Keep watch," Nick instructed them, and he turned his attention back to Gavin. "Did Darius send you?"

Gavin nodded again, and Nick saw the blood seeping through the guy's fingers. He was bleeding out fast, which meant Nick had to hurry to get those answers.

"Who else did Darius send?" Nick demanded. "How many more of your *brothers* are here at the ranch?"

"Just me. It's just me," he repeated in a hoarse whisper.

Nick got in his face. "If you're lying, you won't get in an ambulance. I'll let you die right here."

"I'm not lying. I swear, I'm not." Gavin began to cry. "Darius took Bird with him to go after you and your woman, and we're all that's left of the Brothers."

"Bird?" Nick questioned.

"Barry Gonzales. He went with Darius in the semi."

Nick didn't bother to tell Gavin that Bird was dead. That Darius likely was, too. "All right, I'll call an ambulance," he said.

But there was no need for that. The last breath he'd ever take rattled in Gavin's chest, and he died right there in front of Nick.

"Are there others?" he heard Hallie ask. She had gotten out of the cruiser and was staring at him.

"No. He was the last."

"You're sure?" she asked.

Nick nodded, went to her and brushed a kiss on her mouth before he helped her back into the cruiser. "Let's go see David."

Then, he'd get the ambulance out for Hallie. He doubted she'd feel much pain once she had her baby in her arms, but she'd still need to be checked out.

Nick gunned the engine the moment he was back behind the wheel. It only took him a couple of seconds to reach the house, and the moment he braked to a stop,

Hallie was out and running for the front door. It opened, and Cullen hurried her inside.

Nick was right behind her as they made their way up the stairs. Cullen stayed by the front door, obviously standing guard.

"I just shot and killed the intruder," Nick called down to him. "There aren't any others."

Everything inside Nick told him that was true. Gavin hadn't lied, and the militia was as dead as he was.

Leigh was in the doorway of the guest room, and she stepped aside so Hallie could rush in. "The ambulance arrived at Miller's Point a couple of minutes ago," she told Nick. "Andy's being taken to the hospital, but Darius died at the scene."

Even though Nick had expected Darius's death, he only now let himself feel the relief. An ocean of it. As far as Nick was concerned, the man got exactly what he deserved.

"Vance is on the way here," Leigh added. "Once he arrives, I'm going to the hospital to check on Andy."

Nick didn't think it was necessary to have the deputy stay, but it wouldn't hurt. Plus it might help settle Hallie's nerves. He thanked Leigh, kissed her cheek and went into the bathroom.

Where he saw that the nerve settling was already in the works.

Hallie had David in her arms and was showering him with kisses and hugs. The relief was there. So was the joy and love. David seemed to be enjoying every second of it, too, because he giggled when Hallie kissed him.

Rosa muttered something about checking on Cullen and Leigh, but Nick suspected the woman just wanted to give them a little privacy. Nick might have backed out, too, to give Hallie and David just that, but she took Nick's hand, pulling him into the embrace. David liked that, too, because he latched on to Nick's hair and gave him a gooey cheek kiss.

The moment was perfect.

That was despite Hallie's injuries, Nick doubted she was feeling anything but the love right now. It was the same for him.

"I'm in love with you," he blurted out.

He probably should have waited to tell her that, considering they were coming down from a nightmarish ordeal, but he just couldn't keep it to himself any longer. He'd died a dozen deaths when he'd seen Darius's gun at her head, and now she was safe.

And his.

He caught on to the "his" part very fast when she slipped her hand around the back of his neck and kissed him. Not a gooey baby kiss. This was the real deal. Long, deep and genuine. He could feel the love in it, but Hallie gave him the words he needed to hear.

"I'm in love with you, too," she murmured, and for the first time in hours, he saw her smile. That was genuine and filled with love as well.

David also wanted to get in on that because he grinned and babbled some happy sounds. Nick hadn't needed that as a reminder of what he felt for the boy, but it was good to see.

"He's part of the package deal," Nick told her. "I love him."

Hallie made a sound, a mixture of love, happiness and everything good. And she kissed him again. Nick slipped into the kiss, letting the heat light up all the dark places that the danger had put inside him. But when he finally eased back from her, he knew he had to finish this.

"Darius died at the scene," he told her.

She stared at him a moment, but it didn't take her long to process that. "Good," she said. "Because his death means the danger is really over."

Yep, that was exactly what it meant. Darius had wanted David to cover up his paternity and his part in the black market baby ring. Now that he was dead, there was no reason to come after any of them.

They were safe.

But it was more than that.

"With both of David's biological parents dead," Nick said, "there shouldn't be any hitches in the adoption. In just a few more days, David will be officially yours."

"Ours," Hallie corrected. "Officially David is *ours*."

Her eyes watered. Happy ones, Nick was certain of it. And one day, he'd tell David just how much he loved him. How much Hallie and he had pretty much given him the world.

For now though, Nick gathered them into his arms and just held on.

* * * * *

Look for the conclusion of USA TODAY *bestselling author Delores Fossen's The Law in Lubbock County when* Spurred to Justice *goes on sale next month!*

And in case you missed the previous books in the series, you can find Sheriff in the Saddle *and* Maverick Justice *now, wherever Harlequin Intrigue books are sold!*

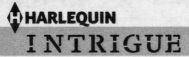
#2121 SPURRED TO JUSTICE
The Law in Lubbock County • by Delores Fossen

When FBI agent Nolan Dalton receives a map from a notorious serial killer, the trail leads him to his ex. Despite the attraction his unexpected reunion with security specialist Adalyn Baxter ignites, danger and passion collide when Adalyn becomes the next target...

#2122 MALICE AT THE MARINA
The Lost Girls • by Carol Ericson

Homicide detective Billy Crouch never stopped searching for his missing sister. When the clues lead him to protect victim Mia Romano, little does he know his beautiful charge is an undercover US marshal, equally determined to locate Billy's sister before mob henchmen silence her for good.

#2123 CLOSE CALL IN COLORADO
Eagle Mountain Search and Rescue • by Cindi Myers

There's a dangerous saboteur on the loose, and Eagle Mountain's search and rescue team is caught in the crosshairs. Volunteers Carrie Andrews and Danny Irwin team up to find the culprit. But will they stop the twisted revenge plot before innocent climbers fall to their deaths?

#2124 BISCAYNE BAY BREACH
South Beach Security • by Caridad Piñeiro

Mia Gonzalez is no stranger to eccentric tech billionaire John Wilson—or his company's groundbreaking software. But when John's program predicts the death of several of the Gonzalez members of South Beach Security, Mia has no choice but to work with him in order to protect her family.

#2125 HONOLULU COLD HOMICIDE
Hawaii CI • by R. Barri Flowers

Honolulu homicide detective sergeant Lance Warner has been haunted by his sister's cold case murder for twenty years. Now there's a possible copycat killer on the prowl in paradise, and reuniting with Lance's ex, cold case expert Caroline Yashima, is his best chance at finally solving *both* crimes.

#2126 SHALLOW GRAVE
by Cassie Miles

When a hunt for an outlaw's hidden treasure in a Colorado ghost town reveals two murdered women, Daisy Brighton and A.P. Carter join forces to investigate. They soon learn there's a serial killer at work. And Daisy has become the killer's next target...

YOU CAN FIND MORE INFORMATION ON UPCOMING HARLEQUIN TITLES, FREE EXCERPTS AND MORE AT HARLEQUIN.COM.

HICNM1222

Get 4 FREE REWARDS!

We'll send you 2 FREE Books <u>plus</u> 2 FREE Mystery Gifts.

FREE Value Over **$20**

Both the **Harlequin Intrigue®** and **Harlequin® Romantic Suspense** series feature compelling novels filled with heart-racing action-packed romance that will keep you on the edge of your seat.

YES! Please send me 2 FREE novels from the Harlequin Intrigue or Harlequin Romantic Suspense series and my 2 FREE gifts (gifts are worth about $10 retail). After receiving them, if I don't wish to receive any more books, I can return the shipping statement marked "cancel." If I don't cancel, I will receive 6 brand-new Harlequin Intrigue Larger-Print books every month and be billed just $6.49 each in the U.S. or $6.99 each in Canada, a savings of at least 13% off the cover price, or 4 brand-new Harlequin Romantic Suspense books every month and be billed just $5.49 each in the U.S. or $6.24 each in Canada, a savings of at least 12% off the cover price. It's quite a bargain! Shipping and handling is just 50¢ per book in the U.S. and $1.25 per book in Canada.* I understand that accepting the 2 free books and gifts places me under no obligation to buy anything. I can always return a shipment and cancel at any time by calling the number below. The free books and gifts are mine to keep no matter what I decide.

Choose one: ☐ **Harlequin Intrigue Larger-Print** (199/399 HDN GRJK)   ☐ **Harlequin Romantic Suspense** (240/340 HDN GRJK)

Name (please print)

Address   Apt. #

City   State/Province   Zip/Postal Code

Email: Please check this box ☐ if you would like to receive newsletters and promotional emails from Harlequin Enterprises ULC and its affiliates. You can unsubscribe anytime.

Mail to the **Harlequin Reader Service:**
IN U.S.A.: P.O. Box 1341, Buffalo, NY 14240-8531
IN CANADA: P.O. Box 603, Fort Erie, Ontario L2A 5X3

Want to try 2 free books from another series! Call 1-800-873-8635 or visit www.ReaderService.com.

*Terms and prices subject to change without notice. Prices do not include sales taxes, which will be charged (if applicable) based on your state or country of residence. Canadian residents will be charged applicable taxes. Offer not valid in Quebec. This offer is limited to one order per household. Books received may not be as shown. Not valid for current subscribers to the Harlequin Intrigue or Harlequin Romantic Suspense series. All orders subject to approval. Credit or debit balances in a customer's account(s) may be offset by any other outstanding balance owed by or to the customer. Please allow 4 to 6 weeks for delivery. Offer available while quantities last.

Your Privacy—Your information is being collected by Harlequin Enterprises ULC, operating as Harlequin Reader Service. For a complete summary of the information we collect, how we use this information and to whom it is disclosed, please visit our privacy notice located at corporate.harlequin.com/privacy-notice. From time to time we may also exchange your personal information with reputable third parties. If you wish to opt out of this sharing of your personal information, please visit readerservice.com/consumerschoice or call 1-800-873-8635. **Notice to California Residents**—Under California law, you have specific rights to control and access your data. For more information on these rights and how to exercise them, visit corporate.harlequin.com/california-privacy.

HIHRS22R3

HARLEQUIN
PLUS

Announcing a **BRAND-NEW** multimedia subscription service for romance fans like you!

Read, Watch and Play.

Experience the easiest way to get the romance content you crave.

Start your **FREE 7 DAY TRIAL** at
<u>www.harlequinplus.com/freetrial</u>.